KT-873-044

SHURI

BY NIC STONE

SCHOLASTIC LTD.

MARVEL

Published in the UK by Scholastic Children's Books, 2020
Euston House, 24 Eversholt Street, London, NW1 1DB
A division of Scholastic Limited

London ~ New York ~ Toronto ~ Sydney ~ Auckland
Mexico City ~ New Delhi ~ Hong Kong

SCHOLASTIC and associated logos are trademarks and/or
registered trademarks of Scholastic Inc.

First published in the US by Scholastic Inc., 2020

© 2020 MARVEL

ISBN 978 0702 30183 4

A CIP catalogue record for this book is available from the British
Library.

Printed by CPI Group (UK) Ltd, Croydon, CR0 4YY
Papers used by Scholastic Children's Books are made from wood grown
in sustainable forests.

2 4 6 8 10 9 7 5 3 1

Book design by Katie Fitch

FOR KALANI JOY AND ALL THE LITTLE BROWN-SKINNED
SUPER-GENIUSES. STEAM ON, LOVES.
—NIC

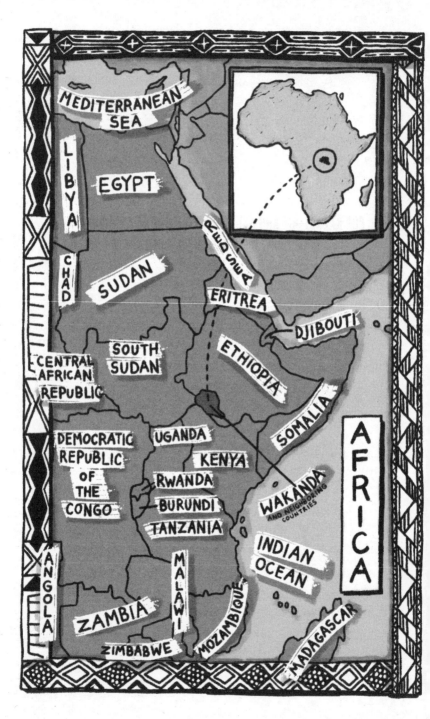

PROLOGUE

She didn't know she'd have to fight.

"Who are you?" she asks, a feeble effort to keep him talking, though she has no idea what that will accomplish. Perhaps her trio of former Dogs of War will happen to turn the corner at just the right moment to come to her rescue . . .

In fact, if you told her a *fight* would be waiting for her the first time she left Wakanda, she'd roll her dark eyes and wave you off like a conspiracy theory (which has no foundation in science).

"Who I am is of no consequence, Princess. The only thing that truly *matters is what I plan to do . . ."*

Not that she'd ever admit it aloud, but she's not even sure she *can* fight. Thanks to Mother, she hasn't truly trained in years. She was still a single digit in age the last time she made a fist.

"And what's that?" Shuri carefully, clandestinely shifts her feet into a fighting stance. Because she has a hunch about what his response will be.

Because fight she will.

"Well, to start, I intend to prevent your return to your beloved homeland."

For herself. Her life.

Her future.

For her people. For *their* future.

She will go out of her way. She will risk it all.

Her very existence.

The princess will *fight*.

For Wakanda.

And with that, his hand shoots out quick as a flash, reaching for Shuri's throat . . .

MISSION LOG

THERE IS SOMETHING FISHY GOING ON.

One week ago, my dear brother stormed my lab *begging* me to make him a new Panther Habit. "This one is too restrictive," he said, holding up the form-fitting catsuit he currently wears as our nation's ruler and protector, the Black Panther. "It hasn't been updated since Baba wore it. Can you *please* make me a new one? And fast?"

I could not have been more excited. I would never tell *him* because it would go right to his watermelon head, but I quite enjoy when T'Challa requests my assistance. Our father died when I was very young, but I think he'd be proud to see his only daughter doing her part to keep our nation safe and secure.

And anyway: The current habit *does* make T'Challa's butt look funny.

I scoured the markets for a . . . *stretchier* fabric. Something with an easy-to-manipulate molecular structure that would bond well with my favorite substance and our nation's most valuable resource: Vibranium. In theory, the correct composition will allow T'Challa to kick high and flip fast, but also absorb kinetic energy from any hits he takes, gather it in the palms of his gloves, and shoot it out as sonic blasts (*FWOOM FWOOM*) that will knock opponents right out of their shoes.

Except nothing is working. *Stretchier* apparently means thinner, and none of the existing fabrics I've tried can handle the optimal amount of Vibranium. I've managed to merge two of the trial fabrics into something new—and sufficiently stretchy—but even this hybrid material can only withstand 73 percent of the total volume of the magic metal in the previous habit. This is fine in terms of shock absorption and turning his hands into cannons, but the 17 percent decrease in bodily protection . . . well, I doubt big bro would be okay with punches and kicks hurting *more*.

My original idea was to distill the heart-shaped herb down to its strength-enhancing, speed-increasing, agility-augmenting essence, and infuse it into the fabric. That way, the longer the material is against T'Challa's skin and he's breathing through the mask, the more powerful and panther-like he would be.

However, the distillation process has proved more challenging than I anticipated.

In the first trial, I created a powder and then attempted to work it into the fabric by kneading. Seemed promising at first, but the moment I stretched it out, a puff of the powder filled the air. I inhaled it and . . . fainted. (Apparently those rumors about the herb taking out the unworthy are true. Bast forbid someone *not* of royal blood catches a whiff.

Also, the powder leaves a dusty film on the skin that makes one's skin appear in dire need of moisturization. And there's no way T'Challa would be okay with looking ashy once the suit retracts.)

In trial two, I tried a vapor. Which might've worked had I not put my head over the flask to check it and fainted again.

Trial three? A gel encased in patches as a suit lining. Thought I'd nailed it with this one . . . But then I tried to pull the piece of test fabric from my arm, and let me tell you: Band-Aid adhesive doesn't have a THING on Vibranium gel patches. *OUCH*.

Fourth and current trial *seemed* a step in the right direction: I lined the fabric with tiny liquid-filled bulbs that would break when hit, delivering small amounts of Heart-Shaped essence to the skin at the point of impact.

And it *does* work—I wrapped a piece around the midsection of a mannequin and gave it a good kick. The liquid *does* release at the point of impact, and *will* coat the skin (maybe even enhancing cell regeneration and creating a speed-healing effect that would prevent pain and bruising? Must test this later . . . In fact, there's a good bit I could test later. Which has me wondering if anyone has ever *studied* the herb before).

But it makes my entire lab reek of rotten fish.

And I just used my last herb bulb.

Frosting on the cake? I have a dead-line now. T'Challa just *appeared* in my lab in holographic form—perks of being able to override any and all security protocols, I suppose—to tell me that he needs the new habit by this Friday. That's five days hence.

Guessing he wants it for our ritual Challenge Day. Which would make sense. There's no telling who will come forward to face off against T'Challa for the throne and mantle of Black Panther, and though T'Challa is *virtually unbeatable*, as he likes to claim, an updated suit would certainly be to his advantage.

Come to think of it, our uncle S'Yan—who

stepped in to fill the role of Black Panther after Baba's death—was wearing the current habit when T'Challa challenged *him* four years ago.

And T'Challa obviously won.

No wonder he wants to be rid of the thing.

Back to the drawing board, I guess.

Wakanda forever.

1

PRINCESS

No sooner than Princess Shuri places her mission log Kimoyo bead into its nest for upload, her mother walks in.

And waves her nose.

"My goodness, Shuri, what have you been up to in here?"

"*Mother!*" Shuri exclaims, darting around the room, collecting flasks and vials and odds and ends in a futile attempt to clear some of the chaos. Despite the lab being a sacred space created just for *her* three years ago as a tenth-birthday present from her darling brother, Shuri knows how her mother, in all her queen-liness, feels about messy spaces. Especially work-related ones. "Did you not see the *Experimentation in Progress* sign on the door? You're supposed to ring the bell!"

Queen Ramonda flicks the notion away as if it's little more than a pesky insect buzzing around one of her elaborate head coverings. Shuri often wonders whether her mother's myriad hats, wraps, and scarves put a strain on her neck.

"I'm serious, Mother! What if I'd been . . . testing the effects of gamma radiation on Vibranium or something? You could've been injured!"

"The only thing that could injure me in this place is the turmoil. Or perhaps the *stench*. Have I not told you, a cluttered space is the sign of a—"

"—cluttered mind. Yes, yes. You've been telling me that since the time I used to dismantle Baba's gadgets in my pre-primary years." Shuri grabs the unrolled bolt of shimmering gunmetal fabric that lies draped across two chairs, the shoulders of a mannequin, and a pile of books, and begins to roll it up. Knocking over an open box of circuits and loose wires with a deafening *CRASH* in the process.

Ramonda's fingertips go to her temples. "Beloved ancestors, why do you vex me with this child?"

"You know you love me, Mother!" Shuri says as she trips on a panther boot prototype and goes sprawling. "Oops."

Queen Ramonda sighs. "Yes. I do." She reaches down to pull her daughter to her feet. "Which is precisely why I am here to escort you to the dress fitting I've no doubt you've forgotten about."

Shuri's smile tumbles to the floor, landing somewhere in the pile of fishy-smelling material. "Dress fitting?"

"My point, precisely. Come now."

"Aww, Mother!"

But it's no use, and Shuri knows it. The queen's word is final. So with a huff and longing glance over her shoulder, she trails her mother out of her favorite place on Earth.

All the way to her *least* favorite place: the glorified oversize closet—with bathroom space—that comprises the queen's dressing chambers.

Queen Ramonda was right in assuming that Shuri had forgotten not only about the dress fitting but the reason for it as well.

Now in addition to being grabbed and prodded and turned and poked like a pincushion ("She's just so *wiggly*," Lwazi, the royal clothier, mutters), Shuri is also being treated to a verbal lashing by the queen mother.

"*How* does the princess of a nation—who is first in line to the throne, no less!—forget about the Taifa Ngao as if it means nothing?"

Mother is pacing. Shuri hates it when she paces. "*Relax*, Mother—*eek!*" Shuri shrieks as she's pin-pricked again.

"I will not *relax*. At least one of us has to take things seriously, Shuri. It isn't as if the tribal elders gather frequently. These meetings are vital for the continued unity and well-being of Wakanda! This particular one especially!"

As Shuri now knows—Mother has been walloping her over the head with it since the moment they'd exited Shuri's lab—there's a council meeting this afternoon. It's the final one scheduled before Challenge Day. During *this* meeting, the tribal leaders will discuss security concerns and other Important Matters.

So fine: It's one Shuri probably should have remembered.

That being said, Mother does seem more *vexed*, as she likes to put it, about things than Shuri feels is warranted.

"Mother, is something wrong?" Shuri asks as Lwazi finishes removing her from what feels like a fabric cocoon and begins to pack his pins, needles, and the like.

"Of course not. Why would you ask that?" the queen replies. As the clothier exits the space, she drags Shuri to a velvet-topped stool at the center of the vast room and shoves her down onto it. "Perfect timing on the fitting. The braiders have arrived."

"The braiders?!" Shuri's arms cross over her head. "But why?"

"Tuh! You think I would permit your appearance in front of the elders with *that* mess on top of your head?"

"There's nothing wrong with my hair!"

"Tell it to the gods," Ramonda replies. "Perhaps they will hear you."

At that moment, three women with luminescent brown skin stride into the room wearing identical bloodred silk robes with matching cylindrical caps. They look, to Shuri, like angels of scalp death. She wishes she had a small vial of heart-shaped herb essence to drop on the floor—there is no doubt the beautiful braiders would all flee from the fishy stench.

"Forgive my impropriety, Mother—"

"I won't have to if you refrain from being improper, Shuri."

The princess huffs. "I was just *thinking* . . . T'Challa has promised to make me the minister of Technology and Advancement in just a few years' time. Wouldn't *this* time be better spent in my lab, building and experimenting and discovering new uses for our beloved Vibranium instead of these—*OW!*—relatively . . . *impractical* aesthetic pursuits? *OUCH!*"

"If the princess would not mind holding *still* . . ." the braider on Shuri's right side says. They have her surrounded: one on the left, one on the right, one at Shuri's back, and Mother standing sentinel in front with what Shuri knows are wildly bejeweled hands clasped behind her.

"Even as minister of Computers and Progress—"

"*Technology* and *Advancement.*" (*Oh, to have a mother who takes my passions so seriously*, Shuri thinks.)

"Yes, that. Even with *that* role, you will still be the sole princess of this nation, Shuri. You are a *royal.* Bast chose to bestow upon *your* ancestor the mantles of ruler and Black Panther. Looking the part is an inescapable aspect of the position."

"But Mother—"

"Don't *but Mother* me, Shuri."

"This *hurts!*"

The queen bends at the waist so she and Shuri are eye-to-eye. "The pain is temporary, my dear." She takes Shuri's arms at the wrist and crosses them over her chest to form an X. "But Wakanda is forever."

As the braiders continue their torture, Shuri's eyes roam the chamber. Above the wall of lighted mirrors in front of her are painted portraits of Wakanda's queens, present and past. Ramonda's is there. Shuri remembers bursting into the room where her mother was perched—with perfect posture—on a tufted, red velvet chair edged in gold. The princess was six years old at most and wanted to show her mother her latest creation: a drone with a Vibranium-centric flight mechanism that used sound waves to stay airborne. The louder the noise, the closer the thing would fly to it.

Which the painter found out the hard way. "OUT THIS INSTANT!" he boomed. And the drone flew right into the still-wet nose of Mother's portrait.

Shuri smiles at the memory, but as her eyes dance over the other queens—everyone is there, from her father's mother to that grandmother's grandmother's grandmother—a little well of disquiet opens up inside her.

Her gaze sticks on N'Yami, T'Challa's birth mother. The woman passed away long before Shuri was born, but Shuri knows that before she married T'Chaka, Shuri and T'Challa's father, N'Yami was the chief scientist of Wakanda.

Did N'Yami step away from her scientific pursuits when she became queen? Did she shirk her lab gear for fancy dresses and glittering jewelry and elaborate headwear?

What about the other queens? Did they have endeavors beyond occupying the throne? It's not that Shuri believes her mother's job is frivolous—she's fully aware of the mental and emotional fortitude necessary to spearhead diplomacy for an entire nation, even one that remains hidden from the world at large.

But what else were queens permitted to actually *do*?

And what of the other princesses? There certainly was no tribute to them anywhere. At least not one Shuri's seen or heard of. How many of the queens looking out over this most *queenly* of rooms in the royal palace birthed daughters?

Had any of *those* princesses been scientists? Tinkerers? Builders of drones with Vibranium flight mechanisms? Clearly their brothers ascended to the throne and took wives, and those wives are the ones featured in these portraits . . . but what of the royal daughters?

Shuri is snatched back into the present as the braider on the left rips through a clump of tangled coils with a fine-toothed comb ("Weapons of mass destruction, those things," she once complained to her mother). The women above her are chattering about Challenge Day. "Do you think anyone will come forward?" one is asking.

"To face T'Challa?" another replies. "They'd have to be mad."

"Agreed. T'Challa is the fiercest Black Panther Wakanda has ever seen."

But the same was said of Baba, and we see what happened to him.

The thought arises in Shuri's head unbidden, surprising her with its sharpness. Its *truth*.

An image of T'Challa holding Baba's Panther Habit in his hand floats before Shuri's eyes.

She blinks it away and returns her focus to the portraits.

Whether or not those women—or their daughters—had active roles in keeping Wakanda safe, Shuri doesn't know.

But she does know one thing: T'Challa requested *her* help.

She has to figure out that habit.

2

COUNCIL

The only thing Shuri hates more than Taifa Ngao meetings is having to wear a dress.

Which means today is a day most blessed for the princess: She's being treated to both.

Due to some strange sewing sorcery, by the end of Shuri's two-hour braiding session this morning, the clothier had returned with a frock draped over his arm that shifted from blue to green to purple, like beetle wings, based on how the light hit it.

The fabric was certainly beautiful—it made Shuri wish she'd been wearing her microscope goggles so she could've examined its molecular structure—but *wearing* the thing was wildly uncomfortable. T'Challa had taught her to be ready for the unexpected, but dresses always required extra work for full maneuverability.

At least it has pockets.

"Stand up straight," the queen mother says as she and Shuri wait outside the doors to the throne room, flanked by Okoye and Nakia, the two Dora Milaje Shuri admires most. (*Why are there no portraits of them in a place of honor?* Shuri wonders. Considering how long the warrior women have been guarding the royal family, it feels like quite the travesty.) Ramonda pushes a knuckle into the divot between two of her daughter's vertebrae in just the right spot to make Shuri's shoulder blades snap together, drawing her up to attention.

"OW!" Shuri cries.

"Much better."

Okoye coughs, clearly to cover a laugh, and the retort that forms on Shuri's tongue is so bitter, she's relieved when the doors begin to open and she's forced to swallow it down.

It's a relief that doesn't last. Because as Shuri takes in the upturned noses and puckered pouts of the tribal elders, who are already seated in the overwrought chairs brought in specifically for these dumb council meetings and arranged in a semicircle with T'Challa's throne at the head, she'd like nothing more than to lift her oddly asymmetrical skirts and *run*.

Her stomach roils and she passes gas instead.

Of course everyone hears it.

"Shuri!" her mother furiously whispers.

"Sorry! It slipped!"

Pulling her*self* together, Queen Ramonda forces a smile.

But then she grabs on to Shuri's arm just above the elbow. And Shuri can feel the dampness of her mother's palm and the slight tremor in her hand.

Something's not right. Shuri's certain of it now.

Also: Where is T'Challa?

"Beloved leaders!" Ramonda purrs in the liquid silk voice she turns on when it's time to remind everyone who's queen.

And it works. Like magic, the storm cloud of tension permeating the space—and causing all the elders to appear as though they are sucking on sour candies (or maybe that's from Shuri's flatulence)—dissipates like a vapor. Even Shuri's shoulders relax a bit. Though she does draw them back up tight to avoid another knuckle poke.

Shuri's 98.3 percent sure she could *never* have that effect on a room full of Very Important (old) People.

"Thank you all so very much for being here with us today," the queen continues as she guides Shuri forward so the two of them can take their seats, Ramonda to the chair that would put her on T'Challa's left, and Shuri to the one on the right. "As you all know, this is our final gathering prior to Challenge Day—"

"Where is T'Challa?"

The question comes from a woman who looks *elder* enough to have been around when Bast chose the first-ever Black Panther. She can't remember the woman's name—or *any* of their names other than Eldress Umbusi, head of the Mining Tribe—but Shuri's pretty sure the lady is of the Merchant Tribe.

No wonder her people are known for being *shrewd* in their business dealings. Clearly, they get right to the point.

The question hangs in the air for a moment and then:

"T'Challa sends his apologies for his absence. He's been called to attend to a rather time-sensitive matter. He did request that I assure all of you of his *readiness* for the impending Challenge."

"Oy, brother. Bigheaded even in absence—" The words have launched off the princess's too-quick tongue before she even realizes they've formed. And the silence that follows them into what suddenly feels like a defiled sacred space—what with T'Challa's chair empty—makes Shuri feel as though a bucket of Vibranium-infused ice water has been poured over her freshly braided head.

But then a man—leader of the Border Tribe if the rhinoceros-head hat is any indication—guffaws. And bursts into laughter. "The girl has a point, eh? Our young king is most certainly not lacking in confidence."

"So very true!" Umbusi chimes in. Now everyone in the room is laughing.

"Perhaps," Ramonda replies. "But it would still do the *princess* well not to speak ill of our king when he is not present to defend himself." She's smiling as well. Which makes Shuri feel better than she'd be willing to admit. "Now if we could move ahead to the reason for our gathering today. I'm sure you all have pressing issues outside the capital that you stepped away from to be here, so we'll keep it brief."

"Hear, hear," crows the River Tribe elder. His loose, shimmery blue clothing flows like water. Which is a bit on the nose if you ask Shuri.

"Per usual, there is no representative here among us from the Jabari-Lands. They remain distant, but peaceful as far as we know, holding to their cultural and religious traditions and continuing to reject our technological advancements."

"Fools," from the Merchant eldress, again wasting no time and pulling no punches.

Not that Shuri disagrees with her. The idea of someone actively *avoiding* technology, and the joy of experimentation that comes with seeking to master it, is further beyond her than pulling off this whole "princess" gig.

"We shall respect our brethren and their chosen way of life so long as it does not interfere with the safety of Wakanda."

"They don't even communicate with *us*," Umbusi says, flicking away any notion of Jabari treachery. "What means of contact would they have with the outside world? The Jabari are harmless. Let us leave them be."

"My thoughts precisely, Eldress," Queen Ramonda replies.

"But what do they *do* up there?" The head of the Border Tribe looks concerned. "What if they are stockpiling resources and building weapons for an eventual revolt?"

"Been watching American films on the PantherTube again, eh, old man?" the River Tribe head says, chiding his friend. Everyone chuckles.

"Perhaps this will be the year they send down a challenger," the Merchant eldress says. "Can T'Challa truly prepare for something he has never seen?"

"I do believe he can," from the queen mother.

Shuri gulps, nervous about speaking up, but struggling to resist the compulsion to defend her brother, especially after her earlier bumble. "As do I. It is part and parcel to the Panther mantle to be ready for anything—"

"Except for the Taifa Ngao." The words are sharp-edged as they pass through the Border Tribe elder's lips, but to Shuri's relief, everyone chuckles. The queen's laughter is forced, Shuri can tell, but it works to temper what could very easily become a diplomacy nightmare. Shuri's fairly sure a ruler skipping out on a meeting with his advisory council would be frowned upon in *any* nation.

"Speaking of the Challenge—"

Another area where the queen mother excels and Shuri falters: regaining control of a conversation.

"—if any of you have warriors who intend to challenge T'Challa for the Black Panther mantle *and* the throne, do remind him of the rules: honorable hand-to-hand combat, no specialized weapons or tactics permitted. And should he succeed in besting our present ruler and protector, ingesting the Heart-Shaped

Herb to prove himself worthy, and receiving the blessing of Bast, will still be required of him."

"Or her," Shuri murmurs under her breath.

"What was that, young lady?" the Merchant Tribe eldress says. (No filter *and* supersonic hearing? Maybe *she* should be the Black Panther.)

Despite having no idea *why* she said it in the first place, Shuri takes a deep breath and repeats herself. "I just said, 'or *her*.'" And she shoves down her inclination to leave it at that. "Because perhaps a female warrior will step forward to challenge."

Now everyone is *really* laughing. Which makes Shuri feel not only angry and stupid, but also powerless.

"Child, the last warrior to challenge a sitting Black Panther was your brother. And after the way he pommeled your uncle S'yan, not a single male warrior in all of Wakanda has had the courage to face him," the Border Tribe elder says. "Our best and brightest female warriors *serve* the Black Panther as Dora Milaje. They don't try to become him."

Shuri's gaze floats to Okoye and Nakia, who are standing sentinel near the doors. If they're bothered by the older man's words, it doesn't show.

This is why she despises these meetings. In addition to being mind-numbingly boring, all these people insist on treating her like a little girl. Shuri is young, yes, but she has certainly contributed to the well-being of Wakanda. Not a single person in the room outside of her mother ever even refers to Shuri as "princess."

Also, it gives her pause that *these* people can't even seem to fathom a female Black Panther. What rhino-head elder said is certainly true: The Dora Milaje have served as Wakanda's royal guard for ages. And they're the best of the best.

Shuri's mind drifts back to the queen's dressing chamber. The lack of tribute to Wakandan princesses. It makes her wonder: Why has there never been a female Black Panther?

"What of the invasion rumors, Ramonda?" The Merchant eldress strikes again. The more Shuri looks at her, the more her bloodred caftan, black jewelry, and pointed hat seem wildly appropriate.

She's certainly got everyone's attention now.

"Invasion?" from Umbusi. "Is this the true reason T'Challa is not with us?"

This time when Shuri glances at her mother, the queen is looking back at her, but quickly averts her eyes.

It feels foreboding.

"I can assure all of you there is nothing to worry about," the queen replies. "Not even the slightest hint of reason for alarm."

No one seems convinced.

"There will be no invasion, so let us lay that rumor to rest," she continues. "Challenge Day shall proceed as normal, and after it has passed, we shall resume our planning for increased fortification—"

"If there won't be an invasion, what need do we have to fortify?" A valid question from the River Tribe elder, though Shuri is irritated at *his* "impropriety" in interrupting the queen.

"Well . . ." Ramonda clears her throat. Which is something she *never* does. No matter how nervous or uncomfortable Mother gets, it never shows. She is the grand mistress of schooled features and an excellent bluff face. Shuri knows *this* from years of mistakingly playing an American game called Uno that T'Challa had brought back from a surveillance jaunt in a city called New Jersey. (What happened to *Old* Jersey, the princess doesn't know.)

"T'Challa should really be the person to tell you all," the queen goes on.

"But you are here and so are we," says Umbusi. "The next Taifa Ngao is four months hence. Wakanda is surely the *most* fortified nation on the planet. We've remained hidden—and therefore *un*invaded, unconquered, and uncolonized—for the entirety of our existence as a nation. If there is need for us to fortify further, all the tribal elders should be privy to *why*."

"Seconded—"

"And thirded," comes the boom of the Border Tribe elder's voice, following that of his River Tribe companion. (Of course the men back one another up.)

The queen mother sighs. "Fine," she says, and everyone seems to pull forward in their cushy seats as if that single word is a magnet.

"I won't say much because it is not my place to speak for the king. But T'Challa has seen and done much during his relatively brief tenure as the ruler and protector of Wakanda, and I believe that, after making our borders as secure as possible, he intends to make our nation's existence a bit less . . . secret."

3

INVADER

Shuri's mind whirls as she makes her way to her quarters after the close of the meeting. All she can think about is . . . Baba. How can T'Challa even *consider* making their existence known to the world? Especially considering what happened.

T'Challa had been just a few months younger than Shuri is now when their father was killed. According to the story she knows, Baba had also considered making the world aware of their small nation. He'd accepted an invitation to some gathering of world leaders, and there was someone there—a man named Klaw—who'd been sent to kill him.

The most troublesome part to the princess: Because T'Challa had been so young, Baba's brother, Uncle S'Yan, had assumed the throne and taken on the Black Panther mantle until T'Challa reached the point where he could challenge him for it.

Shuri is the only other living descendant of T'Chaka. Which would mean if something were to happen to T'Challa, *she* would have to step up. There's never been a female Black Panther before, but what if there has to be? What if . . . it has to be Shuri?

So distracted by these thoughts is the princess, she doesn't realize there is someone in her quarters until she's all the way inside with the door shut.

"*Finally*, you're back!" a girl's (Shuri thinks) voice says. "I was beginning to wonder if I needed to convene a search party."

Quick as a flash, Shuri whips around and extends her arm, palm up, as she makes a fist and lets her hand drop just the slightest bit. A blast of purple light—and electromagnetic energy, though the intruder won't know that until it hits them—shoots out of the bead at the center of her Kimoyo bracelet, and she drops and rolls forward so that she's hidden behind her giant bed.

"What the—OWW!" the voice says. "Uncalled for!"

It makes the princess smile. She'd gotten the idea to arm that bead from a video of a guy who swings around New York City on webbing he shoots from his wrists. *Thank you, spidery guy*, she thinks—

But then there's movement above her—a bounce on the bed—and the next thing Shuri knows, a pair of arms are wrapping around her from behind, one at the neck, and one around the chest, pinning her arms.

Shuri thrashes . . . well, she *tries* to, at least. The person is very strong, and Shuri's too out of practice for her twists and turns to do much of anything.

Though she has to admit: The invader seems shorter than she would've expected.

"A little rusty, eh?" the voice purrs in her ear.

"Let me go!" Shuri barks.

"As you wish . . ." The arms release her, and faster than she can blink, the person has slipped in front of Shuri, grabbed her pulse-shooting arm, and flipped her onto her back on the bed.

A girl's face appears above the princess. Round, deep brown, and set with dark eyes that now sparkle with mischief. "By Bast, you are *dramatic*," she says. "Shooting at me? Really?"

"Oh," Shuri says, the fight going out of her. "It's you." She sits up.

The girl puts her hands on her hips—which are clad in violently bright orange-and-pink patterned trousers. "Well, don't sound so excited!" She's a full head shorter than Shuri, but with athletic curves and muscles the princess is severely lacking. "I'm only your *best* friend in the whole wide world—who's been waiting here for an *hour*, by the way, and who you haven't seen in *ages*—come to invite you on a grand adventure! No big deal at all!"

And she calls *Shuri* "dramatic."

"I saw you two days ago, K'Marah." Her pride crushed, Shuri stands and shucks off the green, toe-squishing, Achilles-pinching contraptions the clothier delivered with her fancy frock. Then she crosses the cool, marble floor to her dressing chamber. She wants *out* of this dress—and away from both the girl and her own embarrassment at being trounced so thoroughly. "And knowing you, whatever 'adventure' you have in mind will be something I want no parts of."

I really want no parts of this so-called friendship, Shuri wants to say, but doesn't. Not that friendship itself is something she shuns . . . not that she'd ever admit it aloud, but the inside jokes and shared fun Shuri has witnessed between girls her and K'Marah's age would be nice from time to time. (Bonus if there's an opportunity to talk science and tech.)

It's just that Shuri's friendship with K'Marah has never felt *real*.

While T'Challa's tenth-birthday gift to Shuri was a laboratory near the Sacred Mound, and access to as much Vibranium as she needs for her technological pursuits, Queen Ramonda's gift to her daughter was a *friend*. "You spend far too much time alone, child," she'd said. "People are beginning to ask questions." (Shuri thought *people* should mind their own business, but of course she didn't say that, either.)

In theory, an arranged friendship isn't *such* a bad thing, especially if the friends genuinely like each other and enjoy each other's company. And it's not that Shuri *dis*likes K'Marah or is *opposed* to her presence. She's just never been fully able to lower her guard.

For one: K'Marah is Eldress Umbusi's granddaughter. Could it be mere coincidence that the princess was given unlimited access to Vibranium— Wakanda's most valuable resource, yes, but also the main item in the Mining Tribe's jurisdiction—on the same day Mother introduced her to the short, pretty girl whose position within the Mining Tribe is akin to Shuri's position in the Wakandan royal family?

Maybe.

But last year when K'Marah began training to become a Dora Milaje, Shuri began to seriously doubt it. (She may also have been a bit jealous, but that's neither here nor there.)

In truth, it's not just the princess-and-princess-protector-in-training nature of the relationship that makes Shuri uncomfortable. She and K'Marah are just so . . . different. Shuri is tall and slim, and hates drawing attention to herself—hence her preference for simple T-shirts and slacks. K'Marah, as evidenced by her neon pants and ruffled tank top, is the opposite.

Also: Where Shuri is grounded, logical, a lover of science, technology, and empiricism, K'Marah thinks more loftily, preferring the "spiritual," as she calls it: the *intangible* and *ethereal*.

Which is precisely why Shuri has no interest in any "adventure" her so-called friend wants to partake in. In fact, the last time the princess allowed the Mining heiress to rope her into an escapade—K'Marah had met some self-proclaimed "spirit scientist" in the market who'd shared a "foolproof" way (using self-hypnosis, which she didn't realize was a thing) to incorporeally project oneself straight onto the Djalia, the plane of Wakandan memory where one can commune with the spirits of the ancestors—Shuri wound up unconscious for six hours, and woke with a splitting headache that required a trip to the royal healers.

"That dress is really stunning, by the way!" K'Marah calls out just as Shuri lets it fall to the floor within her closet space. "The color really makes your melanin pop!"

Shuri rolls her eyes as K'Marah's latest obsession with aesthetics comes to the fore. "Been watching beauty guru videos on PantherTube again, eh?" she shouts.

"I know it's not really your thing, but there's one hair tutorial you *must* watch. I'll send it to your Kimoyo card—"

At the mention of the Wakandan gadget (akin to a "smartphone," as she's heard them called on the internet, but thinner, virtually indestructible, and *far* technologically superior), Shuri's mind drifts off to one of her recent projects: a pair of eyeglasses embedded with the card's technology. The CatEyes will be fully communicative—one can make calls, send/receive messages, etc.—AND will give the wearer instant access to any information a Wakandan could need with the mere tap of a finger. Just the thought sends an excited thrill down Shuri's spine.

"There. I sent." K'Marah has appeared in the doorway of Shuri's dressing chamber with her own Kimoyo card in hand.

Except Shuri's been off in what the queen mother calls "intellectual la-la land"... which means she hasn't gotten dressed.

"Do you *mind*?" she says to K'Marah, ducking behind the mannequin.

(Yes, there's a mannequin in Shuri's closet. As well as a fold-down experimentation station that is presently tucked into the wall. Mother forbids Shuri to spend *all* her waking hours in her lab, so the princess had to improvise. Eureka moments wait for no one.)

"Oh pish posh," K'Marah replies with a wave of her hand and a roll of her eyes. "It's not as though you have anything to *see*." And she walks out.

Despite the sting of the comment, Shuri is thrown back to the Taifa Ngao and the thought of Wakanda's exposure. Because one thing's for sure: While Shuri might be shaped like the River Tribe elder's walking stick, there's definitely plenty in Wakanda to *see*.

And *steal* if you let the head of the Border Tribe tell it.

He was outraged at the very *idea* of Wakanda's existence being revealed to the rest of the world. He spat phrases like *invitation to colonizers* and *pillage of resources* and *utter razing of our land* at the queen mother like poisonous darts. Never had Shuri been more aware of the empty throne at the center of the room.

And never had she been more afraid for her brother—and her homeland.

Another dissenter? That was K'Marah's beloved grandmother.

"K'Marah, may I ask you something?" Shuri asks as she steps back into her bedroom. The other girl is now lying belly-down on the four-poster bed, flipping through Shuri's old textbook on particle physics. Which is missing from the bedside table.

"You just did," K'Marah replies without looking up. "How can you stand to *read* this dreck? It looks like an alien language."

"I'm serious." The princess pulls the book from K'Marah's grip and shuts it with a snap before rolling K'Marah over like a log and taking a seat on the bed beside her. "You've invaded my space. Might as well make yourself useful."

"Well, tell me how you *really* feel, Princess."

"Do you think it would be bad if we weren't hidden?" Shuri continues, ignoring the sarcasm.

"Last I checked, you hide by choice. Which is probably good considering your severe lack of *panache* and tiresome insistence upon 'empiricalism,' or whatever you call it. You could stand to lighten up a bit."

"*Empiricism*," Shuri huffs. "And that's not what I meant."

"So what do you mean?" K'Marah drags herself over to the edge of the bed and sits up so she and Shuri are side by side.

"Our nation. We've been hidden for centuries. Never invaded. Never conquered. Wholly independent. What do you think would happen if other nations knew about us?"

"Other nations *do* know about us, Shuri."

Panic. "What do you mean?"

K'Marah looks at Shuri as though she just asked for the definition of a molecule. "You are aware that we are *landlocked*?"

"Umm . . . yes?"

"And that *landlocked* means 'surrounded by land'? And that the land we're surrounded by is broken up into other nations?"

"Yes . . ."

"Are you under the impression that those nations are unaware of our *landlocked* position between them?"

Shuri doesn't respond this time, but she does see her "friend's" point.

Now K'Marah falls back. "If you *are* under that impression, I can assure you: T'Challa attends every gathering of the Pan-African Congress. And based on some of the stuff he said at the most recent one—"

"You were *there*?"

"Mm-hmm. I've been to two so far. Part of my Dora Milaje training. Anyway, I'm pretty sure your dear brother *wants* more people to know about us."

Shuri's so shaken by K'Marah knowing this first-hand, she can hardly form words. "But what about colonizers? Pillagers? Those who would seek to do us harm?!" There's plenty Shuri doesn't know, but one thing she does: Her father's killer wanted Vibranium.

"I'm not sure the world is as awful as you think, Princess. From what I've seen, the ruler of Narobia is a little off, but no one who knows about us thus far seems to wish us ill. Besides, I'm sure everyone will find out about us eventually. Nothing stays hidden in the age of the internet. Now if you don't mind, I'd love to get to my *reason* for being in your quarters."

Shuri sighs, knowing she's not going to get any further with her personal royal-guard-in-training. And K'Marah's right, isn't she? It likely *is* only a matter of time before they're discovered. Perhaps this is something preemptive on T'Challa's part.

Where is her darling brother? And what could he possibly be doing?

"So are you ready to hear where we're going on our quest?" K'Marah says, clearly oblivious to the magnitude of Shuri's distress.

"I'm not going on any quest."

"Fantastic!" K'Marah sits up and scoots close to Shuri so their sides are flush. The excitement radiating off the shorter girl is so palpable, it makes the tiny hairs on Shuri's arms stand at attention.

Shuri hates it, but now she *has* to know what's going on. "Well?" she asks.

"Ha! Knew you'd come around," the other girl says. Then she drops her voice to a whisper. "We're going to sneak down to the bonfire."

"The what?" Shuri asks.

K'Marah puts her head in her hands. "Bast forgive her on *my* behalf."

"Oh, just get on with it," Shuri says, giving her friend a shove.

"It will never cease to amaze me how little the *princess* of this nation seems to care about our traditions."

"You sound like my mother now."

"Once a year there is a ritual bonfire near the baobab tree, and it is said that while the fire burns, a pathway to the Djalia is opened and the spirits of the ancestors will come down to commune with anyone who seeks their wisdom and guidance."

"Wonder if they can tell me how to fix T'Challa's suit," Shuri mumbles irreverently.

"Huh?"

"Nothing. I won't—" But just before Shuri can get "be doing that" out of her mouth, it occurs to her that accompanying K'Marah to the baobab tree will put her in the perfect position to make a visit to the Sacred Field—the only place in Wakanda where the heart-shaped herb grows—without Mother's knowledge. She needs more bulbs and leaves.

"Okay," Shuri says. "When do we leave?"

4

BROKENHEARTED

Within two minutes of reaching the bonfire, Shuri
regrets her decision to come. She and K'Marah
are both in disguise—in addition to being the
Mining heiress, K'Marah is also the niece of the clothier, which means unlimited access to the royal garment
repository. But the fear of being spotted isn't as easy to
shed as the clothes will be once the princess returns to
the palace.

The air is hazy with what amounts to more vapor
than smoke. Shuri can feel the difference in the moist
coating on her skin and in the way the spicy-sweet

scented substance feels inside her nose. She has no idea what substance is at the center of the blaze licking up from a large crater in the landscape some hundred meters from the baobab tree, but she is *sure* nothing organic—nothing of this world even—could cause *this* mist when burned. It makes her spine tingle.

"Perhaps we should go," Shuri says under her breath to K'Marah as a woman cloaked in serpentine green cloth passes by, shaking a collection of gourds and what look like . . . bones. On strings. "This was maybe a bad idea—"

"Where is your sense of adventure, O Royal One?"

"Don't *call* me that here! Mother will rake me over the holy coals if it gets back to her that I left the palace with no guard!"

"I *am* your guard."

"Not yet, you aren't!"

K'Marah rolls her eyes, but as they continue toward the fire—and into thicker crowds—even she looks more alert. If Shuri didn't know better, she'd say her dear "friend" is looking for someone. "Don't tell me you have a rendezvous planned . . ." the princess says. "K'Marah, I swear to the gods—"

"No, no, nothing like that." The shorter girl rises to her toes (like that helps) and cups a hand over her brow, squinting. She turns her gaze skyward before shifting to look in a different direction, then she jumps once (which does help . . . *Girl's got hops*, Shuri thinks, tugging on a phrase she once heard T'Challa say while watching something called basketball). "Nothing like that at all. Come, let's get closer."

The heat rises as they near the blaze, but Shuri has a sinking suspicion that the increase in temperature has more to do with the increase in bodies wrapped in thick fabrics than with the fire itself. In fact, as she sticks a hand into the air, it feels cooler.

The girls reach an open space and stop. Shuri has to admit, the sparkle, flicker, and dance of the bright orange flames against the ink-dark sky is entrancing.

For a moment, at least.

Doesn't take long for the princess to realize the pungency and harshness of woodsmoke are completely absent from the atmosphere, and as she ponders over the nature of *actual* fire—the combustion-based chemical reaction that permanently alters the molecular composition of whatever's burning—she becomes more and more convinced that *this* fire is . . . scientifically unsound.

"K'Marah, what exactly are they burni—?"

"Shhhh." The other girl, who, despite the grandmotherly frock and hooded cape she decided to wear, looks just like that—a girl—is standing to Shuri's right with head tilted back and arms slightly aloft, palms up. "The plane is open, and the ancestors are near. Close your eyes and lower your guard so you can feel them."

No, thanks, Shuri thinks but doesn't say. And besides, she couldn't close her eyes if she tried. They're too busy darting around, struggling to process everything she's seeing: the U-shaped arrangement of male drummers, all shirtless, but with intricately painted designs all over their chests and arms; the assortment of dancers, some solo, some in groups, all in varying states of bliss; the smattering of individuals either kneeling or prostrate in prayer.

Beyond the bonfire, the baobab tree looks lit from within, and Shuri could swear there are dark shapes, lounging it seems, in the high branches.

A flicker of blue pulls Shuri's gaze to the flames. Then a tongue of green licks up to her right before a swirl of red begins to spin and twist and dance deep within the blaze. And she feels pulled toward it. The only thing keeping her sandal-clad feet rooted in place is the tenuous grip she's able to maintain on *reason*.

"K'Marah, do you see that?"

But the voice that responds doesn't belong to Shuri's friend. Nor does it come from K'Marah's mouth. In fact, Shuri has no idea where the whispers of "*Uya kuvuka*" and "*Sisindisiwe*" are coming from. She does know that their meanings—*She will rise; We are saved*—would be alarming if not for the fact that they feel like sighs of what must be Earth's most pleasant wind breezing over her skin, even *beneath* the dense tunic, pants, and cloak she's wearing.

But then the red flare begins to move. In Shuri's direction.

She blinks, hoping that what she's seeing isn't real, but that just seems to increase the speed of the mysterious light. There are images forming within it now, nebulous at first, but then condensing into what looks like the torso of a woman holding a globe. The whispers shift, and the wind becomes icy: "*Khusela, khusela . . .*" the voice—*voices* now—cry out. *Protect, protect.* Louder and louder, as the red leaps, now panther-shaped, from within the fire and wraps itself around the princess so tightly, it becomes difficult to draw breath.

Shuri's head swims as the smell and feel of *true* smoke—the dry, toxic kind that irritates the airways and prevents the transfer of oxygen to the blood—overtake her senses.

Then everything goes black.

Shuri is hot. Unbearably so. Her mouth is dry, and as she inhales, the air feels so much like sandpaper against the delicate tissues of her throat and windpipe, she wonders if it's better to just not breathe. Something sharp runs over her cheek, and her eyelids snap open . . .

Though she immediately wishes she could shut them again. There in front of her is a woman. Red-eyed and dry-lipped. Dry-*everything*, in fact: The woman's skin is so lacking in moisture, Shuri can see tiny fault lines where it's begun to crack. Like the drought-wrecked landscapes she's seen in her environmental science digital textbook.

The woman lifts a hand, and the globe Shuri noticed before floats above her palm, seemingly lit from within. And speaking of *within*, the more Shuri stares at the glowing orb, the more she recognizes what's inside it: her homeland.

"What . . . what are you doing?" Panic claws its way up the inside of Shuri's chest, more painful than the dry air going down.

And it's warranted. Because the moment the princess looks into her enemy's (she's sure of it) crimson gaze, the woman smiles, revealing jagged teeth, some of which fall from her head as the princess stares, and squeezes her hand shut, crushing the globe—and Wakanda within it—to dust.

Shuri opens her mouth to scream, and cold air rushes down into her lungs.

"Princess Shuri?"

A male voice.

"What are you doing here?"

Laced with panic.

"Does the queen mother know you've come?"

The space comes into focus around her as her vision adjusts to the darkness. In front of her stands a bald man draped in dark fabric, and leaning on a staff carved to resemble a thick vine.

As Shuri realizes where she is—the veiled entrance to the Sacred Field—the priest peeks over his shoulder and turns back to her.

He's petrified.

"You saw her, too?" Shuri asks, too shaken to even wonder how she got here from the bonfire. Though now that she thinks of it—

"Saw who? Did you bring someone else?"

Now he *really* looks scared.

Something's not right . . .

"Are you all right, Priest . . . ?"

"Kufihli." He bows. "At your service, Your Highness."

"Do you . . ." Now Shuri's the nervous one. "Uhh . . . know how I arrived?"

His brow furrows. "I am not sure I understand what you mean?"

How to ask without sounding as though I've lost all of my Kimoyo beads? "Have I been . . . standing here? For very long, Priest Kufihli?"

"Oh no, no! We would not keep the princess waiting! I came as soon as I heard your approach." He takes another worried glance behind him.

So she *walked* here while in the thick of her vision? And where is K'Marah?

Also: Why is the priest beginning to sweat?

"Is something the matter?" Shuri says, attempting to look past him. When he steps to block her view, she *knows* something's up.

She also knows she's dealt with enough unknowns tonight to last her a lifetime. "I need to grab some bulbs and leaves of the herb to run some tests—"

"NO!" He throws his hands up.

"Excuse me?" The statement flows out of genuine bewilderment, but the priest takes it as an assertion of authority.

"I . . . I am sorry, Your Highness," he says with a bow. "I mean you no disrespect. It is just that . . . ahhh . . ." Another wary look backward. "This is not the best time. Perhaps you can return—"

"No, I cannot." *Not without Mother finding out . . .* Which reminds her to get an oath from him that he won't mention her little visit to anyone. "I must gather the supplies now."

And she pushes past, with him calling "*Wait!*" to her back.

Twenty paces into the tree-shrouded space, she sees why: Half of the Sacred Field is dark, the gently phosphorescent leaves of the heart-shaped herb not only devoid of light, but gray and shriveled.

Dead.

She steps forward, instinctively reaching for one of the desiccated plants.

"Don't!" Priest Kufihli catches Shuri's arm before her hand can make contact. That's when she notices the tiny blooms of yellowish flowers dotting the soil like spores of mold.

"What is *that*?"

"We are unsure, Your Highness. We only know that as the plants die, those blossoms spring up in their place." He gulps then. "Another priest, he . . . well, he fell unconscious very shortly after touching those with his bare hand." He points to the mucus-colored blooms. "He had to be revived by a healer, and he—" Priest Kufihli shudders.

"What? What happened?"

"He almost died, Princess. And he still has not regained use of his right arm."

Shuri is speechless.

"We don't know what is happening, but I can assure you that we are working around the clock to find out—"

"How quickly are the plants dying?"

For a moment, Priest Kufihli is silent. Then he sighs. "At the current rate, the entire field will have withered in approximately five days' time."

"Five days?" Shuri blinks, and the image of the dry woman crushing Wakanda flashes behind her eyes. "But the *Challenge* is in five days! If, Bast forbid, someone bests T'Challa, and needs to partake of the herb to gain the Panther enhancements—"

There won't be any herb left.

And more important: If the herb dies out completely, there won't be any for *Shuri* to consume in the event that she has to take up the mantle.

"I will get to the bottom of this," she says.

MISSION LOG

THIS IS VERY BAD.

Thirty-six hours have elapsed since my return to what *should* be Regularly Scheduled Programming, but after the bizarre events of Bonfire Eve, everything feels upside down, inside out, *and* backward.

I have invested the majority of my physical and cognitive resources into attempts at unraveling the herb issue. I have yet to resume the Panther Habit trials—too scared to waste herb juice—but after countless hours of testing and experimentation, I feel further from understanding the root (no pun intended) of the problem than I was when I first discovered it.

Which seems to be the case with every-thing pertaining to that night.

What I know for sure:

1. I had what I suppose was a "vision" (*scientific unsoundness duly noted*) near the bonfire. Whether it was a prophecy or some sort of waking nightmare, I am unsure, but when I regained lucidity, I had traveled three-quarters of a kilometer and arrived at the hidden entrance to the Sacred Field.

2. After making my way past a reluctant priest, I discovered an estimated 44 percent of the heart-shaped herb plants in the field utterly deci-mated by an unknown cause. The dead plants were surrounded by tiny yel-low blossoms that impact the func-tioning of the central nervous system when touched.

3. Upon *exiting* the Sacred Field, I discovered a glaze-eyed K'Marah staring up at the stars. Waiting for me. When I asked her what she was

doing there, she told me that before leaving the fire, I instructed her to meet me just outside the entrance to the field at precisely twenty-two hundred hours.

It was 22:03.

Since our confusing—for me, at least—return to the palace, I have done my best to focus on that which I can control: namely, the herb issue. But every attempt to replant/transplant/dissect/revive the mysterious shrub has resulted in failure.

The liquid essence spoils at precisely the six-hour mark—hello, fishy fragrance!—unless I combine it with something that renders it unconsumable (like foaming hand sanitizer or dish soap, bizarrely enough). I tried encapsulation of both liquid and powdered forms . . . a sort of heart-shaped-herbal pill that isn't shaped like a heart. Sadly, whatever Bast- and/or Vibranium-derived juju that makes the plants so special doesn't play nice with collagen, gelatin, or glycerin:

I wound up with a goopy, burnt-smelling mess that was *very* difficult to get off my hands.

Tried transplanting to different soil. Fail (though this was expected, considering the herb only grows in one location in all of Wakanda). I even tried to figure out what caused the plant death in the first place. Another fail. All I know now that I wasn't sure of before is that the molecular structure of the herb is drastically altered by whatever kills it. The wrecked cells are full of holes and look like they've grown thorns. I've never seen anything like it.

As I said when I began this log: This is very bad.

I've lost a day and a half of work on T'Challa's habit, but this also feels Very Important. And then with . . . what I saw (I guess I "saw" it. "Imagined" doesn't feel correct, though I do *wish* it were some vain imagining) . . .

I'm not sure what to do.

Challenge Day is three days hence. For the *best* possible odds, T'Challa needs a more flexible suit (it would also be great to complete and test the CatEyes prototype to see if it can be fitted inside the habit's head covering, but I might have to back-burner that project at the moment). But even *with* a more flexible suit, there is a chance he could see defeat. Which will mean a new Black Panther will need to be able to partake of the heart-shaped herb.

And as much as I would like to ignore the very much unscientific *feelings* and *inklings* inside my head, I can't shake the image of that desert-skinned woman crushing my homeland within her palm. Especially with the phrase *invasion rumors* ping-ponging around from the Taifa Ngao.

Something is terribly wrong.

I hate to admit it, but I think it is time to speak to Mother and T'Challa.

5
MAYDAY

And Mother is furious.

"You *left* the palace UNGUARDED?"

"Well, technically, the *palace* was very well guarded, which—"

"This is not the time to be *clever*, Shuri!" the queen roars.

All things considered, clever *is exactly what it is time to be*, Shuri thinks, but doesn't say.

"I cannot believe you!" Mother turns on the heel of her bejeweled silk slipper and sweeps toward the door of her chamber, the short train of her fuchsia-and-goldenrod over-robe billowing behind her. Not the most appropriate time for the thought, but Shuri remembers passing her hand over that fabric when she and K'Marah were concealment hunting in the royal garment repository. She'd skipped over this particular vestment because running in the thing would've been impossible. So impractical, Mother's clothing.

"Sneaking out like some . . . common American teenager!" the queen continues to no one in particular.

"Mother, where are you *going*? Did you not hear the rest of what I sa—?"

"We are *going* to speak with the *king*. Come now."

As Shuri jogs to catch up, she hears her mother mutter, "I should confiscate her Kimoyo devices. That'll teach her a lesson."

As the queen and princess pass into the hallway, Okoye and Nakia, both gorgeously clad in their traditional attire, fall into line on either side, and slightly in front of, the two royals.

Which just sets mother off on another tear.

"And you dragged poor K'Marah off into your shenanigans."

Shuri opens her mouth to dispute Mother's incorrect (and fairly offensive—who does she think her daughter is?) assumption, but then she sees their Dora Milaje escorts exchange a glance. And that's when it occurs to the princess how much trouble K'Marah will be in if her trainers knew leaving the palace with the princess had been *her* idea. So she swallows it down. Especially considering how blatantly she's been avoiding the other girl. Shuri's gotten a series of *SOS!* alerts from her "friend" on both her Kimoyo card *and* bracelet, but the thought of adding a K'Marah problem to everything else going on?

No way.

Speaking of which . . .

"Mother, I know you are upset with me, but I received a message from Priest Kufihli just an hour ago. At the rate the plants are dying, there literally won't be any left alive come Challenge Day. If a new Black Panther needs to partake—"

"Are you suggesting that your brother will *lose*?" The queen glares at Shuri so fiercely, the princess feels her face might burst into flame.

"No, no. Not at all—"

"Then cease the dramatics. This matter can wait until the Challenge is finished."

"But it *can't*, Mother. That is what I'm trying to tell you!" They turn left to head up the long hallway that leads to the throne room. "The heart-shaped herb has been imbuing the ruler and protector of our country with superhuman senses and speed and catlike agility and flexibility since the very creation of the mantle! This is an issue of national security!"

Now the queen rounds on the princess, her face alight with rage. "I am fully aware of what the herb *is* and *does*, Shuri. However, no matter how dire *you* perceive this issue to be, there is no excuse for your behavior. Especially not now, with Challenge Day impending and other matters pressing down on us!"

Shuri's skin goes as cold as it did when she was standing beside the bonfire. The drought woman's face arises unbidden and swims behind Shuri's eyes. "Other matters?" she says to Mother, unable to keep the edge from her voice. "What other matters?"

"None that are any of *your* concern," the queen pronounces in that conversation-shuttering way that only mothers can. "You'll forgive me if I find it difficult to believe that our head priest would confide in you prior to speaking with T'Challa or me were the circumstances as critical as you purport. Whatever is happening with the herb, I'm sure it can wait."

And now they've reached the gilded double doors. Per usual, Shuri rolls her eyes as they slooooooowly open.

The princess's heart *does* lift when she sees her brother inside the space, however. T'Challa is standing at the opposite end of the room in front of the massive floor-to-ceiling windows, looking out over his kingdom with his hands clasped behind his back.

"Mother. Sister," he says without turning around.

He thinks he's so cool, Shuri says inside her head. But it does make her smile.

The Black Panther and reigning king of Wakanda is wearing his signature charcoal tunic and slacks (*Does he own* anything *with color?*), and a pair of brown sandals that are glaringly incongruent with the rest of his outfit. K'Marah would lose her *mind* if she saw.

And at the thought of her personal Dora-in-training—which is a sore reminder of the reason she and Mother are here—the princess's joy oozes out of her like sticky paste from a tube squeezed in the middle.

"T'Challa, I have to talk to you," she says before the queen mother has an opportunity to preempt.

To Shuri's surprise, her brother doesn't toss a smirk over his shoulder at her and say *Oh, is that so?* like he typically would.

He . . . sighs.

And a knot forms in Shuri's stomach.

"Your beloved '*baby sis*,' as you like to call her, snuck out of the palace two eves past and paid a visit to the Sacred Field."

Now T'Challa turns around, eyebrows raised. "Alone?"

Shuri can't tell if he's appalled or awestruck. Perhaps a bit of both? She parts her lips to reply but—

"Oh no, no. She took K'Marah with her," the queen mother continues.

And at this, T'Challa *does* smirk. Unlike Mother, the king and Black Panther does know Shuri well. He also knows K'Marah.

"This is not a laughing matter, T'Challa! They could've been seen! Or injured! Or . . . worse!"

T'Challa schools his features, making his expression grave. "You are correct, Mother," he says, fixing a calculated gaze on the princess. "What you did was unwise, Shuri—"

"And dangerous," the queen says.

"And *dangerous*," T'Challa repeats. But there's a spark of mischief in his eye. "You may leave her with me, Mother. I will talk to her," he says.

And the queen buys it hook, line, and sinker. Which irritates Shuri to no end. Why does T'Challa's word seem to carry so much more weight than hers? "Thank you," Mother says to T'Challa with a nod. Then she cuts her eyes at Shuri. "Perhaps the *princess* is more apt to listen to you."

Who's being dramatic now? Shuri thinks.

The queen mother lifts her majestic chin and sweeps from the room with a flourish, taking Okoye and Nakia with her. T'Challa stands stoic and respectful, watching her back as she goes until the moment the massive doors are pulled closed. "Bast, she is over the top," Shuri says, thinking it safe to drop her guard. But then the king rotates away and walks back to his place at the window without the merest glance in his sister's direction. "She's right, you know," he says. "Leaving the palace without a Dora—an *official* one—at your side is extremely unwise. What were you thinking?"

"*Excuse* me? You who used to spend more time traipsing around the city stirring up trouble than seeing to your princely duties?" *Back when Baba was alive*, she doesn't add.

"*While* seeing to my princely duties." He lifts a finger into the air but still doesn't turn around. "There is a difference."

"The only *difference* is that you were a boy and I am a girl."

At this, T'Challa laughs. "Be sure to tell that to the greatest warriors this country has ever seen: Okoye and Nakia."

"You know what I mean, T'Challa."

Now the king does approach Shuri, putting his big hands on her small shoulders. "I do, little sister. And I am aware of how traditional our mother can be. But you must recognize the importance of propriety, especially as a member of *this* family."

Propriety, propriety, propriety. Shuri is really coming to hate that word.

"Now, while I'm certain K'Marah pulled *you* into this youthful jaunt instead of the other way around as Mother believes, I strongly advise against a repeat offense." He continues staring into her eyes as if to show how *serious* he is. (Tuh.) "For the sake of Mother's sanity."

"The heart-shaped herb is dying, T'Challa," Shuri says. "At an alarming rate."

She releases a breath of relief when his expression morphs to bewilderment. "Huh?"

She knocks his hands away. "I 'snuck out' to retrieve more of the herb for the Panther Habit prototype I've been developing. Something is killing the herb, T'Challa."

"Killing it?"

Shuri nods. "I know Challenge Day is imminent, and you surely have a lot on your mind. But . . . well, if more of the herb is necessary, there won't be any left to utilize by the time the Challenge is over."

"I hope you are not suggesting my defeat, baby sis . . ."

Now Shuri throws her hands into the air. "*Why* is that your and Mother's immediate conclusion? *Think* about it: Yes, you took the herb years ago when you"—she waves a hand up and down, gesturing to T'Challa's . . . T'Challa-ness—"became *you*. And no, there hasn't been a successful challenger, or any challengers at all really, during your tenure as sovereign and guardian of our nation. But all that means is that there are unknown variables." *You bonehead,* Shuri wants to add. "As far as we're aware, no Black Panther has ever had to re-ingest the herb, but what if, Bast forbid, you are mortally wounded and need more of the herb to help you heal? What if as you age you *do* need more?" *What if I have to take over for you and I need the herb?*

"Baba would've mentione—"

"You don't *know* that, T'Challa. There were limits to Baba's knowledge just like there are limits to ours. Besides: You were younger than I am now when he died. He probably didn't tell you everything there was to know."

T'Challa's brow furrows.

"Never in the history of Wakanda have we been without the herb. And yes: What if you *are* bested,

Brother? What will the new king do without the enhanced faculties that give our beloved Black Panther the ability to keep us safe? Mother mentioned that you've considered making our existence known to the rest of the world . . . Won't that mean enemies? Who will protect us if the Black Panther is just a regular guy in a stretchy suit?"

T'Challa's eyes flash with anger—though whether it's at the thought of being overcome, or at their mother for revealing his contemplations he surely shared with her in confidence, Shuri doesn't know.

But then his face shifts, and his eyes go wide. Like something has just occurred to him.

"T'Challa?"

He blinks himself back to his center and shakes his head. Then returns to his post at the window, clearly avoiding Shuri's eyes again.

"What are you not telling me, T'Challa?"

"What would you have me do, Sister?" he asks.

"Huh?"

"About this herb dilemma. What is it that you need from me?"

"Oh." In truth, Shuri hadn't really thought that far. What *does* she need from the king? "Well, I've already begun testing so . . . I guess I could use more time?"

"Time?" he says to the window.

Shuri nods then. "Yes. Can you postpone Challenge Day until I get the problem solved? I also need to finish your su—"

But she stops talking because now T'Challa is looking at her like she's grown an additional head. "Surely you jest, Shuri."

"Uhhh . . ."

"We must never shirk tradition."

Just then, one of the Kimoyo beads on T'Challa's wrist lights up and roars like a panther.

Shuri smacks her forehead. "Really, Brother?"

"Shhh," he says, looking suddenly concerned. The king raises his arm to eye level, and a form Shuri recognizes as W'Kabi, son of the Border Tribe elder, appears in front of T'Challa's face like a specter.

"Your immediate presence is needed at the northwestern outpost, my king. We have . . ." The image flickers. "There is . . . something you need to see."

"I shall be there momentarily," T'Challa says. The call ends, and Shuri watches as he shifts to another bead, rubs, twists, and taps it twice, then turns back to the window and slides his thumb over an invisible seam. The pane rises from the floor to right above T'Challa's head, stopping as a sleek, obsidian jet-craft appears outside.

"I have to run," T'Challa says as he steps off the window ledge onto the front of the aircraft. The rounded glass of the pilot capsule slides back the moment his foot makes contact.

Which normally would make Shuri smile—she designed the thing.

But right now, she's too shaken. "So what am I supposed to do?" she shouts over the wind. The vessel moves silently due to its Vibranium composition, but as it hovers she can hear the gentle buzz of the engine.

"Finish my new suit!" T'Challa calls back. As he settles into the seat, an older version of the Panther Habit unfolds around him.

"I mean about the *herb*!"

"I'll have it taken care of!" he shouts. "You musn't forget: Some of the best and brightest minds on Earth reside within our borders!"

"But, T'Challa—!"

"Finish the new habit, all right? I'll handle the rest." Right before the mask overtakes his face, he winks at her. "Together, there is nothing we cannot do!"

6

PRINCESS PROBLEM SOLVER

Together.

Tuh.

Explains why Shuri's standing in the throne room *alone* while T'Challa zips off to handle matters she's clearly being excluded from, right?

She literally stomps—though it makes no sound because her feet are clad in sound-absorbing, Vibranium-soled slippers. Another of her inventions.

Why do he and Mother insist on treating her like some melodramatic child? It's clear that Mother finds the notion of a priest keeping a secret unfathomable.

(Does she also believe the Dora Milaje tell her *every-thing*?) But T'Challa? Shuri expected better from him.

But fine: Since they're both preoccupied, Shuri will take care of it herself. Bast help her, *within* the hyper-limited pre-Challenge time frame. And in doing so, she will prove to Mother and T'Challa—to *everyone*, really—that she's more than just some princess history will forget.

She exits the throne room with what feels like sacred fire crackling in her bone marrow, formulating a plan as her feet pad soundlessly over the marble floors. From what she's deduced so far, something is destroying the plant cells from the inside. Which seems like a simple problem to solve: Isolate the foreign agent, figure out how it's getting in, and find a way to eliminate it.

But it hasn't been simple at all. And after watching T'Challa's vessel shoot toward the storm cloud–filled horizon, Shuri gets a flash of an idea, not unlike the brilliant strike of lightning in the distance, that she hopes will get her one step closer to figuring out *why*.

What every Wakandan primary schooler knows: Thousands of years ago a meteorite made of Vibranium crashed to Earth, creating the Sacred Mound that, to this day, is mined by members of K'Marah's home tribe for the highly valuable substance. Civilization eventually sprang up around it, and now Wakanda, secret bastion of science and technology, exists as one of the most advanced nations in the world.

And something *Shuri* knows as a member of the royal family and descendant of Bashenga, the first-ever Black Panther: The heart-shaped herb's panther-prowess-giving properties come from a Vibranium-rooted mutation that permanently altered the composition of the plant.

But there's more. Something that *hadn't* occurred to her until that jagged shoot of electricity in the sky jogged her memory.

Three years ago, while working on a project for her History of the Wakandas course with a professor so mystical in his leanings that Shuri had a tendency to write off just about everything he said, she stumbled upon the digital archive of an ancient text. Like, words-hand-printed-on-what-looked-like-pages-made-from-the-papery-casing-that-protects-the-pulp-of-the-baobab-fruit type of ancient.

At the time, she chalked the reading up to myth, but now, a piece of it pulses at the front edge of her consciousness, almost like it's radioactive: According to the parchment, ancient Wakandans figured out how to manipulate storm clouds in a way that channeled celestial energies. This—supposedly—created the pathway that pulled the Wakandan Vibranium meteorite down to Earth.

As the princess practically skips back to her chambers, a series of mildly unscientific ideas begin to coalesce in her head. She'll have to leave Wakanda to get to the source of the information she's after . . . but if there's a chance of saving the herb—and her own potential future by extension—it's worth both the risk and extra effort.

Shuri carefully closes her door and rushes into her closet to begin making calculations and gathering supplies.

A check of her Kimoyo card reveals that there are precisely three days, six hours, twenty-seven minutes, and forty-four . . . forty-three, forty-two, forty-one, forty . . . seconds until the Challenge will commence.

Once inside her own travel vessel, Shuri will need approximately eighty-six minutes to reach her destination. Hopefully, it won't take long to make contact with her . . . contact. The princess will explain the dilemma and ask her questions, then get on her way back home with the right answers—or at least some new information that will help lead her in the right direction.

She can depart in the morning and return within twenty-four hours. Which will leave her with just over two days to complete a version of the Panther Habit that will get T'Challa through Challenge Day minimally scathed and with maximum flexibility, and if not *solve* the issue with the herb, at least deduce what is causing it.

So absorbed is the princess in her planning, she doesn't realize she has a visitor until a voice rings out from behind her.

"I take it your conversation with the king was fruitful?"

Shuri, who is kneeling to gather a few items from beneath the normally hidden lab station, startles and pops up too quickly, smacking the back of her head against the underside of the slide-out table.

"OW!" Rubbing the forming knot, she turns to find the queen mother now looking past her at the no-longer-secret science sanctuary.

"What in the name of—"

"The conversation went great, Mother!" Shuri says, closing the space between herself and the queen, then grabbing her mother's hand to pull her out into the open space of the bedroom. "Let me tell you *all* about it."

Queen Ramonda allows herself to be led to the bed, but when Shuri sits and pats the open space beside her—"Join me!" *Smile for effect*—Mother refuses to take the bait.

Crosses her arms instead. "What are you up to, child? And *what* is that . . . contraption inside your dressing chamber?"

"That old thing?" Shuri makes her best attempt at a dismissive wave. "Nothing at all! A small . . . experimentation-site-sort-of thing I built for those early-morning *Eureka!* moments. You know how fleeting they can be. T'Challa sends his regards!"

The queen's eyes narrow, and then she cocks her head to one side and a slight grin tugs at the corners of her mouth.

This is when Shuri knows she's in trouble.

"And where are you going, Daughter?"

A miniature big bang occurs at the base of Shuri's throat, creating a universe of panic she can't seem to speak beyond. She swallows in an attempt to force it down, which only serves to create a spinning, churning sensation in her stomach.

She does manage to hold the gas in this time. "Hmm?"

"The open carry case on your dressing chamber floor you were filling with different items when I came in. Are you planning a trip somewhere?"

"Just to my lab!" Shuri practically shouts, so excited by the validity of the lie, she can hardly contain herself. "I brought those vials and flasks here last week while working on a trial I needed to monitor overnight. I know how you feel about my staying in the lab past curfew. Just trying to fulfill your wishes, Mother."

"Mm-hmm. And the change of clothes I saw?"

Geesh, the woman has the eyesight of an African hawk eagle. "Those are for, uhh . . . in case I spill something! I read somewhere that working in clean clothes is good for productivity. Cleanliness is next to Bastliness, you know!"

"Cleanliness is next to—?" The queen mother shakes her head, but Shuri can see that her blathering is working. "What am I going to do with you, Shuri?"

"Trust me more," the princess says as she rises to gently usher her mother to the door.

"I *trust* that T'Challa impressed upon you the importance of keeping us abreast of your movements?"

"Absolutely," Shuri replies. "One-hundred-and-fifty percent, Mother." *Almost there.* "If I move, there will be a full announcement over the intra-palace communication network."

The queen turns to glare at her. "Do not patronize me, child."

Whoops! Too far.

Thankfully, they're at the door now.

"I think I'm going to call it a night!" Shuri opens her mouth wide in a fake yawn. "Thanks for coming by to check on me, Mumsie!"

The queen mother steps into the hall, and the two Dora Milaje guards posted outside the princess's chambers fall into formation at the queen's sides, ready to escort her to wherever she's headed next.

As they walk away, Shuri exhales.

But then Mother stops.

"Shuri," she calls without turning around.

The princess shuts her eyes. "Yes, Mother?"

"I have your word that you will permit at least one guard to escort you to your laboratory?"

Fabulous. "Yes, Mother."

"Excellent. I will alert General Okoye of your intentions to make the journey. I am *trusting* you to be in contact with her with the details of *precisely* when. Am I understood?"

Shuri sighs. "Yes, ma'am."

The queen gives a curt nod and continues up the hall, away from her daughter and the smoldering wreckage that is Shuri's Save-the-Nation-in-Three-Days-or-Less plan.

Once Mother and her pair of (*unnecessary*, considering they're inside the most fortified edifice in Wakanda) warrior companions disappear around a corner, Shuri turns around, slumps back against her gilded bedroom wall, and slides to the floor like low-viscosity silicone oil down the side of a glass vial.

Except this time when she closes her eyes, she sees the globe of her homeland crushed to dust, and hears an echo of one of the words she heard near the fire: *khusela*.

Protect.

In fact, if she didn't know better, she'd swear someone is whispering it into her ear.

Her eyes snap open, but this time, instead of panic, Shuri feels only the prickling sizzle of determination ghost over her skin.

She lifts her arms, shifts her Kimoyo beads, and taps to call her dear brother.

7

PANTHER

And . . . T'Challa doesn't answer. (Typical.)

Which leaves Shuri with no choice but to camp outside his quarters until he returns from wherever he zipped off to.

It's after ten p.m. when he finally does. He's still in his Panther suit, but without the mask. And he appears weary.

He's also clearly *not* expecting to find his little sister waiting outside his door, looking like she has lit charcoal powder coursing beneath her skin.

He stops dead when he sees her. Then shakes his

head. "I should have known you would be here," he says, nodding at the two Dora Milaje standing sentinels in turn. He pushes the door open, and as Shuri follows him into the vast space beyond, she notices his slightly wonky gait, and how the habit he's wearing . . . rides up in the back.

Looks quite uncomfortable.

So there's no turning back.

"I need your help," she says, pushing past the urge to ask why his shoulders are slumped and what's happening at the border and why it took so long for him to return and if they're going to be invaded. It's not as though he would actually *answer* any of those queries.

"We are not postponing Challenge Day, Shuri. Herb problem or no herb problem, it is completely out of the question—"

"That's not what I mean."

Now he turns to look at her.

Shuri takes a deep breath. "I need you to cover for me, T'Challa."

He crosses his arms. "Cover for you."

"Yes."

"While you do *what*, exactly?"

On the walk over from her own rooms, Shuri decided she'd lean into the lie she'd told Mother: She wants to spend some uninterrupted time in her lab.

She's hoping that because T'Challa gave her the suit task, and she has to be in the lab to complete it, he'll do as she asks and tell Mother there's no need for her "guards."

"I mean, nothing *too* terrible or risky. Just want to work on your suit. That wedgie looks . . ." She cringes for effect. "Yikes."

T'Challa scowls. "Why do you need a cover?"

"Wellll . . . after learning of my visit to the Sacred Field, Mother is watching me more closely. If she had her way, I'd be consistently surrounded by her informants so she can keep minutely detailed tabs on my every movement."

Now T'Challa smirks. "Not too terrible an idea, if you ask me."

Shuri rolls her eyes. "So you'll do it, then? I need freedom to work from approximately zero eight hundred hours into the evening."

He shakes his head. "You know how Mother is, Shuri. I'll request that the guard stay outside the lab so as not to distract you—"

"T'Challa, *please*. The presence of a guard within a one-hundred-meter radius would be distracting. You know how experimentation goes . . . one wrong move triggered by an unexpected sound or motion or *anything*, and *KA-BLOOEY!* The last thing I need while working on YOUR new habit is some sort of intruder-triggered accident." She throws her hands up.

T'Challa merely raises an eyebrow. "You are not making a good case for your request, Shuri."

The princess sighs. "Are you going to vouch for me or not?"

When he looks away, Shuri knows what his answer will be. "What Mother wants, Mother gets, little sister. You know this as well as I do."

"But she will listen to you, T'Challa! There is no way I can *truly* work with a Dora hovering about, watching my every move! This affects you, too, you know . . ."

"I'm sorry, Shuri. New suit or not, I will not oppose Mother so overtly."

So blackmail it'll be, then.

Shuri lifts her chin. She's not the only one who has slipped into neighboring nations without the queen mother's knowledge. "Cover for me, or I'm going to tell Mother where you were really going on those 'covert scouting missions' last year. *And* the year before. I have video and records of your flight paths." She humphs.

For a moment T'Challa is silent. Then: "So you intend to play hardball, eh?"

The princess lifts her chin higher.

"I must admit, I would not have expected such underhandedness from someone like you, Sister."

"I will do what I must for the good of my country."

At this, T'Challa chuckles. Which ignites a torch of rage within Shuri's chest. This . . . *dismissal* is precisely what she must stand in defiance of. She opens her mouth to respond, but T'Challa speaks again: "Take Ayo," he says. "She can post outside the entrance chamber."

"No way," the princess replies. "Ayo is bound by an oath to the throne. You are the sitting king, and she will do as you say, yes. But as you continue to point out, Mother is the queen. If she did as she said she would and instructed General Okoye to have *all* Dora Milaje report back to her regarding my activities, they are bound to do so, T'Challa. No matter which Dora is sent, I'll be monitored more closely than our Vibranium stores."

T'Challa considers this for a moment, then sighs and lifts his arms. "Sorry, Sis. No guard, no go," he says.

His Kimoyo card chimes, and as he checks it, Shuri glances around his surprisingly sparse quarters. Baba had been more extravagant than T'Challa. Gone is the massive four-poster bed with black chiffon canopy. The long, curved leather couch and gold-legged granite table that sat atop the also-missing (synthetic) panther-pelt rug. The pair of larger-than-life-size, hand-carved, black alabaster panther statues that stood sentinel on each side of the room's double doors.

Even the floor-to-ceiling shelves filled with books are gone. ("Better for them to be in the library instead of here collecting dust for the sake of a look," T'Challa had said. And he hadn't been wrong, but still.)

The difference in the space gives her a chill. She tries not to think about it too much, but Shuri misses her father. She has a hunch Baba wouldn't have been opposed to her learning hand-to-hand combat and gaining proficiency with various weapons. Undergoing the same rigorous study-and-training regimen as T'Challa had.

Especially since she's first in-line to the throne.

Perhaps it's wishful thinking, but standing in this room, remembering the way her father would launch her into the air above his head and catch her, how excited he'd get when she'd come to him with something she'd built from the little click-blocks she loved to play with as a child, Shuri is *fully* convinced Baba would be behind her in this.

She has to make *him* proud.

Time to bring out the big guns. "I won't have a Dora stationed outside my lab, T'Challa."

"Then perhaps you won't be spending as much time

there as you'd like. Frankly, there isn't much Mother can do about my past indiscretions, so your threat is without impact, and, therefore, without power."

Shuri locks and loads. "Okay," she says with a shrug. Then aims and . . . fires. "Guess I'll just have to tell Nakia how you *really* feel about her."

T'Challa's eyes go wide. "You wouldn't."

"Oh, I absolutely would. Remember that night you drank a bit too much pineapple wine at Eldress Umbusi's birthday party, and I had to assist you?" Shuri reaches into the pocket of her tunic and produces a single Kimoyo bead, which she drops into her bracelet. The moment she taps it, T'Challa's voice fills the cavernous space. *"She is more beautiful than the baobab plain at sunrise. More delightful than the pulp of a ripe mango. She smells better than—"*

"Okay, okay! Stop it!" T'Challa says, and Shuri smiles as she shuts the bead off.

"Quit your *grinning*," he continues. "You will have six hours."

"Six?" That won't work for her *true* plan. At least two would be eaten by travel, and once you add an additional half hour on each end to *prepare* for travel, half of the allotted time is gone. "But that's not enough time!"

He shrugs. "You want more time, take a guard."

"I won't be able to truly focus!"

They fall into silence.

But only for a brief moment. Because then T'Challa's face illuminates like an LED filament light bulb.

And in that instant, Shuri knows precisely what he's going to say.

"No . . ." she begins just as he shouts the exact thing she's hoping he won't:

"K'Marah!"

8

MOBILE

Based on the generic *"K"* response Shuri received on her Kimoyo card when she sent K'Marah a text message asking if she would fill the role of "lab assistant" the following day (*"and wear trousers,"* the message said), she's expecting K'Marah to arrive at their meeting point cool, calm, and collected.

She does *not* expect K'Marah to burst into her quarters *before* sunrise, and squeal like a tickled piglet as she somersaults through the air, and lands perfectly on her back in the bed as if she'd slept that way. She turns her face toward the princess, smiling as though the entire scenario were the most normal thing in the world. "Hi."

"You're not serious," Shuri replies, squeezing her eyes shut in hopes that when she opens them again— at least an hour from now—she will find herself alone and discover that *this* was nothing more than a terrible dream.

But then there's another high-pitched squeal. And her bed begins to shake.

Because K'Marah is pounding her arms and kicking her legs like a jittery pre-primary schooler.

"K'Maraaaaaaaaaah!"

"I am so *EXCITED*!" K'Marah practically screams.

"Can you keep it down?" Shuri says, walloping her friend with a pillow. "Let's not wake the entire palace!"

"Okay, okay." K'Marah flips onto her side to face the princess, and props her newly cornrowed-and-beaded head on her hand. "So when do we leave?"

The hairs on Shuri's arms rise to attention. K'Marah couldn't know they're *actually* leaving, could she? "I know for a fact that I instructed you to meet me beneath the Panther effigy at the city gates, in trousers, at eight thirty." She looks K'Marah over. "Not only are you wearing a ridiculously impractical *dress*, it's— Time, please!" Shuri says to the air.

The vaguely robotic reply is instantaneous: "The time is zero six hundred hours and twenty-three minutes."

"Six twenty-three?!" Shuri exclaims, shoving K'Marah's shoulder.

"I'm sorry, I'm sorry!" K'Marah flops onto her back and sighs. "I couldn't sleep! I brought clothes to change into, just wanted to look like myself as I came to your quarters—"

Shuri gasps and grabs K'Marah's arm. "How'd you get into the palace?" She turns her head, wide-eyed. "Were you questioned?" Yes, T'Challa talked Mother out of sending a Dora Milaje with Shuri to the lab, but as far as she knows, there is a leather-clad warrior woman just outside the entrance to her chambers. Raising *any* kind of red flags would be disastrous.

K'Marah shoos the panic away. "I took a transport car and came to stay with Uncle shortly after receiving your message last night. Ayo let me in here."

Shuri doesn't respond to that. Even though she does feel a certain *way* about this pseudo-friend of hers having such easy access to the palace.

The shorter girl leans closer and lowers her voice to a whisper. "So what are we *really* doing?"

Oh boy. "What do you mean?"

"The whole lab thing is a cover, right? If I know anything about you, it's that you prefer to work alone. So if you're asking me to be your 'assistant,' there is definitely something else afoot." She taps Shuri's nose.

Shuri is too stunned to respond.

K'Marah grins and returns to her back. "Whatever it is, I can't *wait!* I figured you'd be awake by now because . . . well, you're *you*. But at any rate, we're both up, yeah? Why not get an earlier start?"

The princess groans and throws an arm over her face, but she's unable to deny K'Marah's logic. Besides, the sooner they leave, the more time to gather information. Hopefully.

"Fine," Shuri says.

And she gets up.

Getting out of the palace earlier than Shuri reported to Mother proves a hair more difficult than Shuri expects. The Ayo part is easy: By the time Mother is awake, and the Dora has told her of the girls' predawn departure "to the lab"—with T'Challa's blessing—they'll be en route to Kenya and it'll be too late for the queen to thwart Shuri's plan.

Slipping past the intensely stoic palace guards, though?

And they do have to *slip* past: While it would take fire, flood, or falling bombs for Ayo to wake the queen, the palace guards would instantly report Shuri's movements. And Mother would have her and K'Marah held until she could storm from her chambers and interrogate Shuri.

No thanks.

"Okay, so the plan . . ." Shuri says to K'Marah as the shorter girl finishes the laborious task of tucking her hair into one of the classic caps the market boys wear. They're in the cloakroom near the delivery entrance to the palace, now dressed in the sand-colored garb of male Merchant apprentices.

"Bast, these clothes are itchy," K'Marah complains.

"No great deed was ever done without discomfort." Shuri cracks open the door to the hallway and peeks out. "As I was saying, we need to disable three guards." She squats to rifle through the purple velvet bag at her feet, pulling out a few items and transferring the rest to a less . . . *conspicuous* bag. One that fits their disguises. "Catch," she says, tossing K'Marah a smoke-colored orb about the size of a yellow passion fruit.

"What is this?" the mini-Dora asks, holding it up for examination.

"That," Shuri replies with a grin, "is phase two." She turns back to the cracked doorway and squats, something held loosely in her hand. "Okay, so the security cameras will be playing looped footage for the next ten minutes. Here's what's going to happen: First, I will release a beetle-bot—"

"A *what*?"

"You'll see. Then you will roll that stink bomb out—"

"Stink bomb?!" K'Marah looks at the thing in her hand like it's grown tentacles.

"Stop interrupting! Those two *should* do the trick, but if not, phase three will take out the electricity on this hallway for approximately four-point-three-two seconds. I'll lead us out with my thermal imaging goggles."

"Thermal imaging gog—you know what, never mind. Let's get this over with."

As K'Marah—and the wildly unprepared guards—come to discover, a beetle-bot is just that: a robot shaped like a giant flower beetle.

When guard two notices the thing crawling up guard one's trouser leg, he screams . . . and then kicks.

"Yikes!" K'Marah says as guard one goes down, the fake bug still making its way up toward the man's head.

"Phase two!" Shuri whisper-shouts. K'Marah depresses the little button on the stink bomb as Shuri instructs. Then quick as she can, she rolls the thing into the hallway.

Shuri instantly shuts the door and yanks one of the cloaks down to stuff beneath it. "It's very potent," she says to K'Marah.

And then there's a *THUD*. The girls look at each other, but neither speaks.

After a few breaths of silence from the other side of the door, Shuri taps one of her Kimoyo beads, and a glowing countdown leaps into the air. "Thirty-three seconds until the air is clear," she mouths to K'Marah, who shrugs and mouths "*What?*" back.

When the time has elapsed, Shuri carefully removes the cloak from beneath the heavy door and hangs it up. Then even *more* slowly pulls the door open. A hazy, shimmering mist coats the air. The girls wave their noses, though the smell has mostly dissipated.

But then they both stop. "Uhhh . . . Shuri?" K'Marah asks as she takes in the scene. Before them lie three dark green heaps. The guards, one of whom has what looks like a palm-size bug perched on his cheek. "What exactly was *in* that thing?"

"Hydrogen and ammonium sulfides with just a pinch of methane . . . basically the fragrance that would come out of a big man who'd eaten spoiled luwombo. Which . . . maybe I overdid the methane?"

She steps over to guard one to remove her mechani-bug from his face, and gives his leg a little shove with the toe of her boot. He's out cold.

"No need for phase three, I guess?" K'Marah says.

The girls glance at each other wide-eyed and then explode into giggles.

"Let's go," Shuri says.

Within ten minutes, the two girls-dressed-as-boys are passing through the city gates.

"Shuri—" K'Marah begins, but the princess cuts her off.

"Shhh!" Shuri hisses, peeking behind them to make sure they aren't being trailed.

No one even looks twice as they each move through the waking city with dingy brown rucksacks full of clothes and supplies slung over one shoulder. While Shuri forced K'Marah to leave behind most of the froufrou foolishness she'd brought to take on the journey—drapey tunics and patterned silk skirts—K'Marah *did* convince Shuri that she should pack one dress, just in case.

They will be interacting with royalty, after all.

After a couple of minutes of silent trekking on the side of a paved road used solely for weekly transports of Vibranium from the mines to the city, K'Marah takes a look around and then turns to Shuri with the light of many suns dancing in her eyes.

"Uhhhh—" the princess begins nervously, but that's all she gets out because K'Marah whoops so loudly, a flock of starlings launches into the air from deep within a field nearby.

"K'Marah!"

"Shuri, we *made it*! Can you believe it? We made it out in broad daylight with everyone moving about the palace! This is next-level!"

And as much as Shuri wants to shush her now-prancing friend again, she also can't help but smile.

They *did* make it out.

"We are rather enterprising, eh?" Shuri says, giving herself a mental pat on the back.

Her joy does not last, however. Not five minutes later, the girls crest the hill that will lead them down to the baobab plain, which they have to cross to reach Shuri's lab just outside the Sacred Mound, and discover that the plain is occupied.

"Whoa!" Shuri says, grabbing K'Marah's rucksack to pull her down so they can't be seen.

Both girls poke their heads up just enough to see the gathering below. T'Challa stands, in full Panther garb, at the head of what looks like some sort of *Taifa Ngao: War Council Edition*—instead of the heads of the various tribes, a group of Wakandan generals, as evidenced by the glint of the newly risen sun off their telltale golden sashes, is gathered in a circle. Eleven men, plus Okoye, plus T'Challa. A baker's dozen of warriors including the king.

"What do you think they're talking about?" K'Marah whispers.

A number of terrifying topics a war council would need to discuss flash through Shuri's head, but she manages to spit out something less dire: "My guess would be the impending Challenge Day. Perhaps they are discussing security measures. The plain *is* where the whole thing will take place, so it would make sense to meet there, yes?"

"You tell me, Princess," K'Marah replies.

Just then, T'Challa's head lifts, and Shuri knows for a fact that despite the distance—and the mask—her dear brother is looking into her eyes. It makes her breath stick right beneath the hollow of her throat.

"You know," K'Marah says, "not to be all harbinger of doom, but I get the distinct impression they are *not* discussing Chall—"

"Time to move," Shuri says, refusing to allow full vent of K'Marah's thought into the atmosphere. "We can talk about it later, but for now, we need to get out of here."

By the time they reach the mound—after an additional twenty-five minutes trudging largely at a slant around the field—the cloudless sky has become a curse, and both girls are sweating buckets from the sun beaming down on them without mercy.

They both flop to the floor once inside the cave-like entryway to Shuri's lab. "Welcome to my Innovation Domicile," the princess says, her eyes shut and chest heaving.

"This is it?" K'Marah replies. "*This* is your glorious laboratory?"

"Technically this is the mouth of the cavern that *leads* to the ID. It's down there through those doors." Shuri drags her arm into the air to point, then lets it drop.

"Is there water inside?" K'Marah asks.

"Of course."

"Then let's go." K'Marah climbs to her feet and lifts Shuri up, pulling one of the princess's skinny arms across her own shoulders so the pair can walk in tandem. "I'm on the brink of death from thirst."

"That hyperbole feels wildly inappropriate considering the danger of our imminent undertaking."

"Which you still have not told me about . . ."

"We'll get there, I promise."

The girls slog up the uneven rock floor of the nature-carved hallway, and once in front of the real entrance to the lab, Shuri slaps her hand against a palm scanner. K'Marah looks on, agog, as a purple laser light runs from the tops of Shuri's fingertips down to her wrist and back again.

And when the clouded glass doors slide open and a disembodied female voice—which sounds suspiciously similar to the queen mother's—proclaims, "Welcome, Princess Shuri, Ancient Future, Enlightened One, First of Her Name, Heir to the Throne, and Future Black Panther," K'Marah, now fully alert, turns her widened eyes to her best friend.

"Oh really, now?"

"Shut up."

As soon as they're through the doors, K'Marah does just that.

For a moment, at least. "Holy—"

"K'Marah!"

"Sorry, I just . . ." Shuri watches her friend's eyes roam around what amounts to the lab's foyer. One wall is covered in soundproof foam (experimentation with Vibranium often involves loud noise), but all the others are made of the same thick glass as the entry doors. In a curved arc around the space lay three separate test areas where the princess executes her actual experiments.

"Impressed?" Shuri says, reveling in K'Marah's inability to lift her unhinged jaw from the gleaming epoxy-resin floor. They make their way past the smart boards and cabinets filled with bits and bobs, and approach an open, though darkened, doorway. The moment Shuri steps within a foot of the room, a light clicks on inside, revealing a small kitchen.

"I mean, *wow*," K'Marah says. Shuri reaches into a miniature cooler—run on Vibranium, of course—and hands K'Marah a small glass bottle of water. Then she uncaps one for herself, and gulps it down.

After opening a few cabinets and pulling different snacks from within to add to her rucksack—dried hibiscus calyxes and mango slices; rice crackers and a variety of hard cheeses—Shuri turns to a still-stunned K'Marah. "Ready?"

"Uhhh . . . I think so?"

Now the princess can't stop smiling. "Right this way." She heads toward what looks like nothing more than a wall. But then she lifts her wrists and taps one of her Kimoyo beads.

A hidden panel lifts straight up into the air, revealing a walkway into a dimly lit space beyond.

And when the girls get to the end of it and the automatic lights come on, Shuri doesn't stop K'Marah from letting her curse fly this time.

In front of them hovers a relatively large, but undeniably sleek . . . mode of transport. Faintly shimmery and obsidian in color, the vessel gives the appearance of a gargantuan panther midleap—head tucked, both sets of strong legs extended, and long, lithe body outstretched in a perfectly curved line. Just without the tail.

"The shape is for aerodynamics," the princess says, "because there are two modes." She taps one of her Kimoyo beads, and a pair of sleek wings extend out from the belly region.

"But what . . . is it?" K'Marah begins a slow walk around the perimeter of the thing, her awestruck gaze dancing over its lustrous surface, but not daring to touch it.

"It's how we're going to get out of here," Shuri replies. "There's more. Let me see your Kimoyo bracelet."

K'Marah holds her arm up in the air.

Shuri shakes her head. "No, silly. As in *give* it to me?"

"Oh . . ."

K'Marah does, then watches, baffled, as Shuri runs to the far side of the room and puts it on the floor before jogging back.

"Check it out . . ." Using her own bracelet, Shuri shifts and taps one bead, which makes the panther vessel rise higher into the air, and then when she rubs the top of a different bead, a whitish beam-looking thing shoots out from under the vessel and wraps around K'Marah's Kimoyo bracelet—which then comes flying at them.

"Aah!" the shorter girl screams, blocking her face.

"Sorry!" from Shuri. She reaches out and snatches the soaring jewelry from the air. The beam vanishes. "Still working out the remote kinks. It'll be smoother from the control panel inside. It's basically a tracking apparatus that utilizes the Kimoyo signal—and can fetch. I call it Kimoyo Capture."

"And when would you need something like that, exactly?" K'Marah asks, still shaken, as she takes her bracelet back and places it on her wrist. "Planning to lose your bracelet in the woods or something?"

Shuri shrugs. "You never know." She lowers the vessel back down. "Lastly, watch this . . ."

Shuri removes her Kimoyo card from a pocket, taps around on the screen a few times, then lifts the device to eye level and flicks the top edge of it forward as though tossing something from the card into the air.

And K'Marah gasps. Because right there before both her and Shuri's eyes, the vessel vanishes over the course of about ten seconds: from the outstretched front paws, up over the head, and down the body to the point where the tail would be. Now K'Marah *does* reach out, and as her hand connects with what looks like vaguely warped nothingness—"BAST, this is *amazing*, Shuri!" she says—a little heart-shaped bloom of some unexpected emotion bursts open inside the princess.

Why does Mother never react this way?

"I, umm . . ." And Shuri has to swipe at her eyes and clear her throat before she continues. "I've been working on something for T'Challa, and while doing some research on twenty-first-century superhero garb, I stumbled upon a secret organization in America called S.H.I.E.L.D. I went into their digital design archives looking for garment inspiration, and found the schematics for something they call a helicarrier. The flight technology was very impressive. So I . . . borrowed it. And made upgrades."

K'Marah spins to face Shuri, a look of stunned disbelief etched into her raised eyebrows. "Shuri, are you a *hacker*?"

"What?" Now the princess can't meet the other girl's eyes. "No, I . . . I mean, I put the details of the mirrored cloaking mechanism I added into the file as a form of payment—"

"You are totally a hacker!" K'Marah, beaming, bounds over to Shuri and wraps her in a tight hug. "I am *so* proud of you!"

"You're ridiculous, let me go."

K'Marah does with a chuckle.

"Anyway, as I was saying—" Shuri lifts her Kimoyo card again and flicks it back toward herself as though summoning something from a distance. The vessel comes back into view. "This is how we'll be getting where we're going." *Completely undetected, hopefully.*

"Fabulous!" K'Marah replies, bouncing on her toes. "What do you call it? You *have* given it a name, right?"

Shuri smiles. "This"—she gestures to the vessel— "is the *Panther Mobile*."

"Uhh . . ."

Now she turns to K'Marah. Beaming. "You and I, future Dora, are going to Kenya."

MISSION LOG

WE MADE IT OUT—THAT IS *AFTER* MY "BEST FRIEND" LAUGHED IN MY FACE UPON HEARING ABOUT WHAT I CALL MY PERSONAL TRANSPORT VESSEL. SHE INSISTED THAT I CHANGE THE NAME OR SHE WOULDN'T BE STEPPING FOOT INSIDE IT (WE SETTLED ON THE *PREDATOR*).

But our skyward sailing certainly was not *smooth*.

Note: I must make some caliber and ballistic adjustments so that the vessel will make sharper turns, and the shifts in flight angle won't be so jolting. K'Marah experienced more nausea than I would've expected on our admittedly turbulent way through the forest.

Speaking of which: There is definitely something amiss in my beloved country. I fought hard to convince myself that my assertion above the plain was the truth—that the generals were gathered to discuss the final preparations for Challenge Day.

But our forced reroute—I couldn't risk flying *over* the plain, even while invisible, any more than we could've waltzed across it, especially with Okoye there (*informant!*)—revealed some other troubling oddities.

We went through the mechanized security forest on the southern border with Niganda, and I was able to use my Kimoyo beads to control the trees and create a wide enough path for us to pass through—up to a point.

Then we were attacked by a small grove. Of trees.

It shouldn't have been that surprising: The forest was designed to hide Wakanda from aerial view and to prevent intruders from getting in.

But I wasn't expecting the branches to begin lashing out and shooting laser beams at *us*. Especially since I should've been able to override them.

The first blow was like a slap on the *Panther Mobile*'s—excuse me, *Predator*'s—rear that shot us both forward and sideways. "Whoa!" was all I'd been able to manage. The laser caught us on the side. This time, the *Predator* herself spoke up: "*Warning, damage sustained to left flank.*"

Once I regained my bearings, I was able to dip, dodge, and maneuver around the arboreal swings coming at us, and even fire off some kill shots of my own (so glad they were mechanical), but once we were through that rough patch, I noticed some other . . . abnormalities.

For one, along our path, I had no problem distinguishing the natural trees from the mechanized ones—largely because a number of the natural trees were lacking their typical vibrancy. In fact, as we closed in on the border itself, we passed a cluster of trees that were glaringly dead. The trunks were the brooding dark gray of angry storm clouds, and the branches gnarled and leafless. And I can't be completely sure because we weren't close enough for a concrete observation, but it seemed the entire deceased copse was spotted covered with a strange yellow, like some giant had upchucked all over it. It was almost as though they were covered in mold spores . . . not unlike the soil around the dead heart-shaped herb plants.

Then once *through* the forest and officially in Nigandan airspace (without permission, oops), we passed over what looked like a small encampment about half a kilometer from the border.

Which I would've thought inconsequential had it not triggered an alarm. *"Warning: vessel detected,"* claimed the incongruously dispassionate mechanical voice. Which made my skin prickle as though covered in spiders.

Because being "spotted" should've been impossible. We were in *full* Invisi-mode, which not only involves the mirroring technology that mimics the appearance of the surroundings, but also a series of

Vibranium silencers that create a small vortex of soundlessness around the *Predator*, making its movement undetectable to the human ear.

We should've been invisible *and* inaudible.

Not only undetectable, but also untraceable.

Which now makes me wonder: What *was* that encampment, and who does it belong to? Wakanda or Niganda?

Or someone else? Are the Nigandans allies, or would they wish us harm?

And what is happening to the trees? Is it the same plague that is destroying the heart-shaped herb? Will it slowly eat away at our forests as well?

I *must* get to the bottom of all this.

Here's hoping my next log has more answers than questions.

9

TURBULENCE

And now Shuri can't relax. The flight to Kenya is approximately one hour and twenty-six minutes in duration—twenty-three of which have already elapsed—and the princess *should* be working on both acquiring permission to land, and finding someone to alert the queen of Shuri's intensely impromptu impending visit.

But every time she blinks, she sees the image that popped up on her security screen after the alert rang about the *Predator* being detected in flight: the head and shoulders of a man with his head tilted back and his hand against his brow, shielding his eyes. The picture is colorless and grainy (*note: Upgrade the vessel's security cameras*), but Shuri can see that he was wearing dark sunglasses and a solid-colored kufi cap on his head.

And if the tilt of his chin and the direct frontal shot of his face in the photo are any indication, there's a good chance this mystery man *did* see the *Predator* as it flew overhead.

But *how*?

T'Challa called shortly after they crossed the border, and although Shuri quickly deflected with a text message about being in the thick of a fabric test, he'll definitely call again. And she'll have to mention what she saw.

But what exactly will she say?

She peeks at the image of the man again—it's still glowing in the bottom-left corner of the console screen—and huffs.

"Will you sit *down*?" K'Marah grumbles from where she's reclined on one of the fold-down, fully adjustable beds in the open space behind the cockpit. She's "recovering" from the motion sickness she claims to have experienced on the ascent, but it hasn't escaped Shuri's notice that K's had a Kimoyo card in her hand since they reached ten thousand feet in altitude.

Said card chimes with an audible buzz of vibration, and K'Marah giggles in a very *un*–Dora Milaje–like manner.

Which sets off a different set of alarm bells in Shuri's head.

"K'Marah, who are you talking to?" she asks.

"Hmm?" K'Marah swipes and flicks and taps away . . . and then raises two fingers in what Shuri recognizes as the American hand gesture for *peace*, and snaps a photo of herself.

"WHO"—now the princess rises—"are you talking to, K'Marah? And what are you telling them?"

"Don't *loom*," the other girl says, sticking an arm out to prevent Shuri from getting too close. "If you *must* know, I'm talking to a friend."

"Named?"

"What difference does it make, Shuri? It's not like you *know* him."

Him. "So it's a boy?"

"Bast, you're worse than Okoye. AND Grandmother."

"This is serious, K'Marah! What if this *boy* is using the IP address of your Kimoyo card to track our geo-location? Does he know you're with me?"

K'Marah rolls her eyes, then shifts her focus back to her device. "Are you planning to be this way for the *entire* trip? If so, please take me home—"

The Kimoyo card slips from K'Marah's grasp as Shuri plucks it out of her hands.

"Excuse me!" the shorter girl cries, leaping to her feet.

Which makes Shuri take a step back. Yes, the height advantage is hers, but the princess is under no illusions about who would win *this* fight. Again. She almost hands the thing back just to avoid any escalation. But . . .

No. This is important. Tantamount to their safety—and that of Wakanda, in fact.

Which as a Dora in training, K'Marah should know.

So she stands up as straight as possible. "K'Marah, I need for you to tell me the truth. We are risking more than you know by going on this trip." (It's more than Shuri knows, too, but of course she doesn't say that.) "And I'm not referring solely to how *grounded* we will both be if my mother or your grandmother finds out about it. Not only are our lives at stake, the welfare of Wakanda is, too. As a rising Dora, you're supposed to be as dedicated to the security of our country as I am."

Now K'Marah huffs and crosses her arms. "You're such a killjoy," she says, turning her face away and dropping back down onto the bed.

"K'Marah—"

"If you *must* know, his name is Henny," K'Marah continues, unprodded. "We 'met' on the message thread of a PantherTube video about Krav Maga—"

"Krava *what*?"

"My word, you are hopeless." K'Marah shakes her head. "It's a form of mixed martial arts developed for the Israeli Defense Forces. Henny made a rather insightful comment about something in the video, and so I commented on his comment, and he commented back, and so I commen—"

"Okay, I get it," Shuri says. The *Predator* wobbles just the slightest bit, and Shuri peeks over her shoulder at the autopilot readings to make sure they're still on course. (They are. And the radar readings look good, too. They should be smooth sailing into Kenyan airspace within seventeen minutes or so.) "So you had a conversation. Then what?"

"Then nothing," K'Marah says with a shrug. "I haven't met him in person and don't really intend to. I only know he's Jabari because he told—"

"He's *Jabari*?! Are you out of your mind?"

"You know, to be first in line to the throne, you sure do sound prejudiced. The Jabari are Wakandan, too."

If the princess *could* turn red, she'd be the bright crimson of a lithium chloride flame. "That's . . . not what I meant." (Though of course it is. Could she have meant anything else?)

"Yeah, okay."

"And," Shuri says as a justification light bulb clicks on inside her mind, "let's not forget: They may be Wakandan, but the Jabari have chosen to cut themselves off from the rest of us. They don't submit to our rule." *They* are, *however, still permitted to challenge the sitting sovereign for the throne.* And Shuri supposes that *does* make it a good idea to be nice . . .

"Oh, boo-hoo."

A plume of rage balloons up inside the princess, and temporarily turns her vision the color of blood. "This is precisely why I *didn't* want to bring you! You're so flippant about everything!"

She watches the words land, punching not only the smugness but also the excitement right out of her friend's face. And instantly, Shuri wishes she could take them back.

K'Marah . . . crumples. "I'm sorry, okay?" she says, turning away. "It won't happen again."

Shuri's eyebrows pull together. There's a quaver in K'Marah's voice now that she wasn't expecting.

Then K'Marah sniffles and swipes at her eyes.

Now Shuri is *really* nervous. And not entirely sure of what to do. Her area of social expertise is with artificial intelligence, not crying best friends. "K'Marah? Are you okay?"

And the shorter girl sighs. Heavily. "I'm not sure I'm cut out for this, Shuri."

"What do you mean?"

"This Dora Milaje thing. Part of the reason I said yes to you was to get a break from all that. I want to be a Dora, yes. But I also want to be a kid. Who goes on fun adventures. With *friends*."

"Oh."

"I overheard some of them talking about me," K'Marah continues. "A few of the older trainees." And now she looks up at Shuri. "They said I'm 'too flippant.' Same way you just did. That I'm only there because of Grandmother's position. That she got me in. That part's not true: I worked and trained hard, and tested well. But what if they're only allowing me to *stay* because of who Grandmother is?"

Shuri doesn't immediately respond to that.

It's not like she doesn't understand where K'Marah is coming from. She opens her mouth to say something comforting—*I mean, I'm not exactly* princess *material, am I?*—but then there's a *BUMP* that jolts the *Predator* so intensely, both girls are knocked sideways.

"*Oof!*" Shuri exclaims.

K'Marah clutches her stomach and drops down

onto the edge of the fold-down bed. "Oof, indeed—"

There's another bump.

"Is that going to keep happening?" K'Marah says, now stretching back and draping an arm over her face. Shuri notices an ornate, charcoal-colored, glass-beaded bracelet beside K'Marah's Kimoyo one. Of course the glamour girl managed to add *something* ridiculous and impractical to her drab Merchant's apprentice getup.

Another bump.

Shuri completely loses her balance this time, and stumbles into the passenger cockpit chair. "It shouldn't be happening at all—" She breaks off to carefully make her way into the captain's seat.

And once she does, and her eyes alight on the weather radar screen, she's *very* glad to be sitting already.

They're not merely headed straight into a storm—one that was wholly absent when Shuri looked not ten minutes ago. It seems the storm is *trying* to engulf them.

Which can't be right.

With a slide, swipe, two-finger rotate motion, and *tap tap tap* on the navigation touchscreen, the princess makes some quick adjustments to the altitude level and flight path. It won't pull them completely out of the tempest, but they'll skirt the edge of what would be the most turbulent portion.

Then her gaze is pulled back to the weather radar screen . . . and she watches in combined awe and horror as the storm changes paths as well.

"This is not happening," Shuri mutters under her breath.

Another bump. "Get strapped in, K'Marah," the princess says as she does the same. "If you need to remain in a supine position, there are harness components that pull out from the sides of the bed."

K'Marah just groans.

"I'll do my best to dodge the worst parts, but things are definitely about to get . . . bouncy."

And bouncy they do get. In fact, the whole experience brings to mind some American thing called pinball that Shuri learned about in her Foreign Cultural Studies course just this previous quarter. Except *that* is a game, and *this* . . . certainly isn't.

Her Kimoyo beads light up, and a robotic, but oddly soothing, masculine voice fills the cabin: "T'Challa, aka Big Head Brother, is calling."

Shuri has zero intentions of answering, of course—he would totally *hear* the turbulence with his hypersensitive, heart-shaped-herb-enhanced auditory capabilities, and would no doubt have a cattish conniption—but knowing he's calling *does* shake a memory loose in the princess's mind.

T'Challa a few years back, sitting at a random table in the palace kitchen. Awestruck and chuckling and munching on plantain chips. "You girls are really something," he'd told her with a shake of his head. "I go to surprise the stunning apple of my eye, and almost lose my life as a result. Can you believe that?"

Shuri hadn't answered.

"I tell you one thing, baby sis," he'd gone on, "if you ever decide to fly over Kenya, brace yourself . . ."

That's when she slows the vessel to a complete stop, shifting into hover mode, and smacks the button on the dash that will make them fully visible and alert anyone in the surrounding area to the *Predator*'s full surrender.

Almost immediately, the storm begins to retreat on the weather radar screen, and the livid gray skies all around the girls and their high-tech, flying cat-ship dissipate.

Shuri exhales.

When the clouds right in front of the *Predator* part to reveal, not another plane, but a *person*, Shuri smiles. Apparently the girls won't have to find Shuri's contact: *She* just found them.

"Whoa," K'Marah says as she makes her way

forward and takes in the brown-skinned woman dressed in black, with white hair and flashing alabaster eyes, who has emerged in front of them.

Floating. In midair.

"Who is *that*?" K'Marah continues.

For a moment, Shuri doesn't say a word.

And when she does finally speak? It's barely above a whisper: "That," the princess says, "is Queen Ororo."

10
HEAT

At Ororo's instruction ("Wait, *Storm*? As in the X-Man . . . well, X-*Woman* Storm? You *know* her?" K'Marah said once she'd put two and two together), Shuri lands the *Predator* on the outskirts of a village a handful of kilometers inland from the city of Mombasa. By the time the girls disembark, Ororo is flanked by two very muscular men in T-shirts, tan shorts, and sandals. They've assumed a royal guard–like stance: feet planted marginally wider than shoulder width, hands clasped behind their backs with arm muscles flexed, chins slightly elevated.

"Okoye would lose her *mind* if a Dora Milaje showed up for duty dressed so casually!" K'Marah whispers as the girls approach their hostess. "Maybe I should request to transfer here . . ."

"Will you shush!"

"I'm just saying!"

"My dearest Shuri!" Ororo says once Shuri and K'Marah are within hearing distance. "What a pleasant surprise!" She spreads her arms and Shuri walks into them.

"Unbelievable," K'Marah gasps from behind.

This makes Ororo laugh. "And who might you be?" She releases Shuri and steps forward to extend a hand to K'Marah . . .

Who is frozen in place. Her eyes flick down and lock onto the Kenyan queen's extended hand, but she doesn't budge.

"You can shake it," Ororo says with a smirk. "Since you're a friend of my favorite princess, I won't electrocute you. This time."

A tinny squeak escapes K'Marah's throat, and everyone (except for her)—bodyguards on *chill* included—bursts into laughter.

"Ororo, this is my friend K'Marah—"

"Her *best* friend," K'Marah says, suddenly back to herself. "It is an honor to meet you, Ms. X-Woman

Lady Storm." She grabs Ororo's hand and gives it a firm pump.

"Ororo is fine, dear. And that's, uhh . . . quite a grip you have there."

"Oh!" K'Marah pulls her hand away. "Sorry!"

Shuri smiles to herself. She could get used to this bumbling idiot version of her "best friend."

"Come, we'll go into town." Ororo gestures for them to follow her. "Your aircraft will be safe here."

The girls comply—after Shuri puts the *Predator* back in Invisi-mode (can't be too careful)—and trail the white-haired queen and her guards to an open-topped truck propped up on overly large wheels. Once everyone's inside, the man in the driver's seat uses an actual *key* to crank the engine.

"Does this use *petrol*?" The incredulous question comes from Shuri this time.

They get underway, and again, Ororo laughs. "We don't all have *Vibranium* to power our cities and fuel our vehicles, you know."

"Wait, you know about Vibranium?" K'Marah sounds more panicked than Shuri realized possible.

"Ah, so the princess hasn't told you how we know each other," Ororo replies.

"I met Ororo through T'Challa," Shuri says. "She was—"

"Your king's first crush," Ororo says, looking as proud as a freshly preened peacock. "Don't tell him I told you, but I *rescued* T'Challa from a group of Vibranium-thirsty would-be colonizers when we were around your age."

(*If you let T'Challa tell it, he's the one who rescued her*, Shuri thinks.)

"Whoa . . ." K'Marah breathes, enamored anew.

"So, yes, I have full knowledge of Wakanda's store of the precious celestial resource. But you can trust that I would never do anything with the information that could bring harm to your beloved nation."

They bump along the dirt road in silence for a couple of minutes. Then a cluster of small man-made structures pokes its head above the horizon just as K'Marah says, "Is it toasty here, or is it just me?" before slumping down in her seat and shutting her eyes.

And Shuri must admit: She's not wrong. While the princess doesn't seem to be quite as impacted as her friend, it *is* hot. And much drier than she would've expected considering the location's proximity to the Indian Ocean.

They pull into the city proper as Ororo responds: "We have experienced quite the shift in our average temperatures over the past few ye—"

There's a loud ringing noise like an old-school fire alarm going off, and Shuri jumps. She and K'Marah exchange a nervous glance.

But then Ororo pulls out a heavy-looking device from a hidden thigh-pocket of her rather snug trousers. Speaking of which: She wonders what the weatherwoman's outfit is made of. It's clearly quite stretchy and seems to be moisture-wicking as well because good ol' Storm doesn't have a lick of sweat on her exposed arms, chest, or abdomen despite the blistering heat.

She makes a mental note to ask.

"This is Ororo," the incongruously blue-eyed woman says into the handheld item. So it's a phone. She winks at Shuri, but then her expression shifts and she shakes her head and pinches the bridge of her nose. "Again?" She sighs. "Fine. I'm coming." She hangs up, then puts a hand on the driver's shoulder. "Q, drop me at the greenhouse. This accursed heat wave has caused the atmospheric regulator to overheat, so I'll have to reset the spaces manually. Again."

"Would you like for us to accompany you?" Shuri says, jumping at the chance to assist her personal heroine. "I'm sure I can reset the regulator and, with the right tools, make some tweaks to the mechanism that will prevent it from overheating again."

"That's very kind of you, Princess, but I've got this one covered. Such is the beauty of being able to manipulate an ecosystem." She winks as the Jeep—that's what Shuri heard a guard call the automobile they're in—pulls to a stop in front of a low, glass edifice: The entrance is at the middle of a domed central building abutted by two longer sections that sit like arms extended out at its sides. Turning back to the driver, Ororo continues, "Deliver these wonderful young ladies to Yasha. She's at the station. I'll let her know they're coming."

She hops out.

"Girls, I'll be back with you shortly," Ororo says before shoving the door shut. "Lickety-split, like a lightning bolt." Then she gracefully spins away from them and jogs up the walkway to the building.

Yasha is younger than Shuri expects: only a couple of years Shuri and K'Marah's senior.

She's also . . . rather grumpy.

"But *why* would Moe saddle me with *guests* when she knows I'm in the midst of *extremely urgent* research?" she grumbles while leading the two younger girls through the halls of a small brick building about a kilometer from where they left Ororo.

"Wow, she sounds just like *you*," K'Marah whispers to the princess.

"She does *not*," Shuri hisses in reply. "Who's *Moe*, do you think?"

"Why don't we ask?"

"She doesn't seem the type to look kindly on—"

"Excuse me, Yasha?" K'Marah practically shouts. "Who is this Moe you speak of?"

The Kenyan girl heaves an intensely exasperated huff and looks at the ceiling as if to say, *WHAT have I done to deserve such imbecility in my presence?* "M-O-E," she says, pronouncing the letters. "Mistress of the Elements?"

"Ah."

"Not to be a nuisance, but will we be permitted to sit soon?" K'Marah goes on, very much being a nuisance. She wipes her visibly damp brow, and her mismatched bracelets click against each other. "I'm feeling a bit faint."

Yasha forcefully exhales another puff of irritated breath. "Two more rights, and a left, and we'll have reached the dining hall. I've been instructed to provide you with sustenance, and then 'keep you company' until Moe is no longer occupied."

"Well, don't sound so excited . . ." Shuri says.

"I most certainly am *not* excited!"

"Not too quick on the uptake, either," K'Marah quips. Which draws a snort from Shuri.

"We'll be out of your hair soon, Yasha," the Wakandan princess says in an attempt to smooth things over with the Kenyan girl. "I know what it's like to be interrupted midtask and can understand your frustration."

The building they're in, as it turns out, is the Meteorological Research Center of Haipo, Kenya. And Yasha, at age fifteen, is the chief researcher. "My primary focus at this juncture is the effect of global climate change on East African nations, specifically this one," she tells Shuri and K'Marah over sumptuous servings of ugali and nyama choma.

"It is certainly *hot* here," Shuri says in between bites of food. "In fact . . . K'Marah, I wonder if you're experiencing heat exhaustion. We haven't exactly stayed hydrated."

"No idea," K'Marah replies. "But I'll admit: I'm astonished by just *how* much hotter it is here than back home. Yes, we're slightly closer to the equator. But man. Doesn't it seem *unnaturally* hot to you?"

"Where is 'home'?" Yasha asks.

"Wakan—OW!"

"Shhh, K'Marah," Shuri says through gritted teeth.

Yasha's fork stops halfway to her mouth. "You're from Wakanda?"

Now the princess glares at her guard-in-training. Then sighs. "Yes," she says, "we are."

To Shuri's shock, Yasha goes from prickly . . . to ice-cold. Flat mouth, narrowed eyes, the whole deal. "I see," she says. With undeniable bite behind the words.

Makes the princess feel as though she's jumped into a pool filled with shards of broken glass. "Why . . . do you say it like that?"

"Oh, no reason," Yasha replies with a shrug. "Though now I understand why you're so shocked by the heat here."

"You do?" This from K'Marah.

"Of course," the other girl goes on. "With all your advanced technology and your surely shiny climate-controlled buildings and homes, a drastic change in outdoor temperature must be little more than a blip on the radar for people like you."

Shuri can't think of a single word to say. "Well, I mean—"

"Many of your neighbors resent you, you know. Not we here in Kenya, obviously. Moe is *clearly* fond of your king." She forces a smile. "But there are . . . others. Who feel you Wakandans are self-centric and elitist."

Now K'Marah rolls her eyes. "How would *you* know how 'others' feel?"

"I am the Kenyan rep for the East African Climate Change Caucus," Yasha says. "Wakanda, of course, has no representative, but *all* of your surrounding nations—Niganda, Azania, Narobia, Canaan, Uganda—certainly do. As I mentioned, with the way you hoard resources that could benefit all, environmental concerns don't seem to be an issue for *you*, but they are for your neighbors."

"I—" Shuri begins to respond, but Yasha's mobile device buzzes on the table.

"Hello?" the older girl says, answering eagerly.

From the respite that slides down Yasha's face, smoothing her brows and cheeks, and dismantling the tension in her shoulders, Shuri knows their time with the cantankerous girl is up.

Which is a relief, yes . . . but also leaves the princess with the feeling of something vile laid over her skin. *Has* the climate changed markedly in Wakanda? Isn't this something she should know?

One of Shuri's Kimoyo beads illuminates to alert her to a new incoming message, so she removes her card from her pocket to read it in text instead of having the bead play it aloud.

It's from Priest Kufihli. "Fifty-eight percent and steadily spreading." Shuri gasps. Whatever's killing the herb hasn't slowed.

Two and a half days left.

Yasha ends her call. "Eat up," the Kenyan girl says, clearly thrilled to be almost free of her Wakandan burdens. "Moe—Ororo—is ready for you. And I need to return to my research."

11

STORM

There's no way to know for sure, but Shuri has a hunch Ororo has her and K'Marah delivered back to the greenhouse and brought inside so they get the chance to see good ole *M.O.E.* in action.

Without being trapped at the center of it, that is.

The girls can hear the *crack!* and *ba-BOOOOM!* of a thunderstorm as they follow one of the guards across the domed area at the center of the building. The greenhouse is significantly larger than it seems from the front, and the princess was incorrect about its presumed shape: There aren't merely *two* long arms attached to the central dome. There are five. The building is shaped like a half sun.

And as they approach the section at the center, Shuri can't help but smile: The hygrometer/thermometer combo gauge just outside the door indicates that the air within the room is dry and the temperature is too hot. But the princess is certain that's about to change. And she and K'Marah are going to witness it.

"Stay here at the observation window," the guard tells them (like they'd do anything different). "Queen Ororo has almost completed her task and will be right with you."

Then lightning flashes.

"Great Bast," K'Marah whispers, thunderstruck.

Within the greenhouse room before them, Ororo—*Storm*—is hovering midair with her arms outstretched and one leg bent slightly at the knee. An airborne ballerina wrapped in black. Her eyes are wide and bright as if the sun lives behind them, and her white hair billows and crackles around her, perfectly contrasted with the brown of her skin.

Shuri's not sure what plants are being grown in that particular room, but she watches, rapt, as Storm brings her hands toward each other in front of her and moves them in opposing circles like she's pedaling a bicycle with her arms. A wispy, white cloud forms between them, and when she's satisfied with it, Storm pulls her hands apart, then pushes them back together, spreads them wide, then brings them tight again . . . shaping, stretching, molding.

For the grand finale, she floats around the room, depositing the handmade cloud in long, wispy sweeps over the various lengths of plants. And by the time she's back on the ground and walking toward the door, the humidity streaks have gone from white to invisible.

Shuri takes another peek at the temperature and humidity measurements on the meter as Storm steps through the exit, definitely beaded with perspiration this time. Both readings are in the "ideal" zone now.

"You're like a goddess," K'Marah proclaims to Ororo as a guard passes the beautiful older woman a towel.

Ororo wipes the sweat from her brow. "A mutant, actually. But close enough." She grins at them. Now a hint of mischief flickers in her back-to-blue eyes. "Follow me."

She leads them down a corridor that runs alongside the greenhouse she just exited, and through a door that leads out back. They cross a short plain of dead grass that shushes underfoot and are soon climbing the porch stairs of a small cottage.

Shuri exhales with relief the moment they step inside: It's blissfully cool.

They've entered the kitchen. "Have a seat, loves," Ororo says. "I'll grab us some beverages."

The girls sit—well, K'Marah more *flops down*—at a wooden table positioned beneath a window that gives a view of the greenhouse complex a short distance away. Shuri thinks again of the plants inside it. Of the veritable magic Ororo just wrought on the *actual* atmosphere to keep those plants alive.

Why couldn't things be that simple for *her*? Walk into the Sacred Field, swirl the air around, and boom: Whatever's killing the herb would be instantly rooted out, and the plants would spring back to life right before her very eyes.

The gentle *thunk* of a glass being placed in front of the princess brings her back to reality. Ororo pulls out the third chair and lowers herself into it with more elegance than Shuri knew possible for such a basic act. Feeling bizarrely chastened by some inner voice, the princess pulls her shoulders back as discreetly as possible.

K'Marah, with much less discretion, bolts upright as if yanked by a string.

Ororo lifts her glass. "Drink up," she says before doing the same. "I know you both must be parched."

And she's right. So they do.

"Now," Ororo continues, setting her own glass down after an extended pull of the contents. "What can I do for you loves?"

"Is this your *house*?" K'Marah blurts, finally alert enough to take in the surroundings.

Shuri sighs and shakes her head. "Really, K'Marah?"

Ororo's eyes sparkle with delight as she fixes her gaze on K'Marah—who looks like she's about to combust beneath the force of the Mistress of the Elements' full attention. "Sometimes, yes," Ororo says. "Occasionally, it's nice to exist in a state of simplicity. People underestimate the value of *home* as a place of stability, where things subsist in a particular order and there's a rhythm your heart beats to." Now she turns to Shuri. "What has thrown your sense of home out of order, *dada*?"

Dada. Sister.

Despite the pulsing, sparking tangle of questions and worries in Shuri's head that seem to have grown multiple heads and legs, the princess exhales. "We are having some . . . vegetation issues," she says, risking a glance at K'Marah. It's not like she told the other girl exactly *why* she needed to come to Kenya. Does K'Marah even know about the herb and what it does? Is the princess about to blow some closely guarded royal secret?

Why does everything suddenly feel so tenuous?

She takes a deep breath. "There's this plant. As far as I know, it's unique to Wakanda. Has its origin in some sort of chemical reaction that suffused the space between the plant's cell walls and cell membranes with Vibranium."

Ororo nods. "The heart-shelled shrub, or some such, yes?"

"Heart-shaped herb," Shuri says. "But close enough."

"Ha! I get it!" K'Marah exclaims.

Shuri and Ororo both turn to her, expectant.

"You know, because earlier I called you a 'goddess' and you said 'close enough' and now Shuri is saying 'close enough' to you? Well played, Princess." She shoves Shuri's shoulder, and Shuri just puts her head in her hands.

"Well played, indeed," Ororo says without a hint of annoyance. (*How does she do it?* Shuri wonders.) "Continue if you will, please, Shuri."

"Well, the herb is dying."

Ororo's white brows lift, and something loosens in Shuri's chest. She clearly knows enough about the herb to recognize the gravity of the situation.

"Yes," Shuri says. "And fast. Just before we were brought back to you, I received a message from the head priest letting me know over half of the plants are dead."

"Whoa," K'Marah says.

"Indeed. Something is causing the Vibranium bonds to disintegrate, which irreparably damages the cell wall," Shuri continues as all the data she's collected thus far begins to scroll through her mind like the credits at the end of an American film. "Problem is, I can't seem to find any evidence of a foreign substance— other than the Vibranium—in or around the cells themselves. And I've tried every reparative measure I can think of. I've grafted the stalk of a dying herb to a living one, stimulated accelerated cell division, attempted to reestablish the Vibranium bond during mitosis—"

"Welp, you've totally lost *me*," K'Marah says with a yawn. "I'm taking a nap." And she puts her head down on the table.

Shuri shakes hers. "Are *you* following? I know I can get a bit carried away with the 'science-talk,' as T'Challa likes to call it . . ."

Ororo puts a reassuring hand on Shuri's forearm. "I do follow, love. Just not entirely clear on why you felt coming to see *me* would prove beneficial."

Another deep breath. "Well, that's the thing. I found records of an old . . . supposition, I guess you could call it. It purports that there were ancient Wakandans who learned to . . . do what you do." The princess nods her head in the direction of the greenhouse. "They would manipulate cumulonimbus clouds, and through this manipulation, shifted some celestial energies and created the path to Earth for the Vibranium meteorite."

"Huh." The corners of Ororo's mouth are pulled down in what reads to Shuri as *intrigue*, but she's still nervous about her next question: "Does that . . . sound like a thing that's possible, considering *your* abilities?"

"Anything is possible, my dear."

"You can say that again," comes K'Marah's muffled voice from where she's burrowed her face into her crossed arms on top of the table.

"Now, can I say *I've* used storm clouds to rearrange the cosmos and pull some otherworldly element from the sky? Sadly, no."

This makes Shuri smile.

"But I won't say it can't be done. Considering all the variables involved, it makes as much sense as any other explanation for cosmic phenomena that affect us here on Earth."

Now the princess has gone all starry-eyed.

"Don't talk nerdy to her, Ms. Ororo Storm," K'Marah says, lifting her head to prop her chin on her hand. "She'll fall in love with you."

"Oh, will you shut *up*?"

Storm laughs again, but it doesn't bring Shuri any joy this time. "I just need to figure out what's *wrong*," Shuri says to no one in particular. "I thought that maybe since Vibranium might've come to us through some storm cloud–controlled galactic gateway, perhaps *you* would know more about how that works. And if there was a way to use a similar mechanism to—ugh, I don't know!"

And she truly doesn't. In fact, the longer Shuri sits here in Ororo's sweet and simple little kitchen, the dumber she feels for coming. What did she think would happen? Ororo would kick into Storm mode, do some thunderhead sorcery to open a cosmic energy funnel, and suck the solution down, vacuum-style, from wherever it's waiting in the universe to be found?

Ororo's warm brown hand lands on Shuri's bare arm. Her nails are polished white. "While I'm sorry I don't have the solution you're seeking, Princess, I *can* assure you that no interdimensional space portals have opened recently, and nothing extraterrestrial has entered the Earth's atmosphere. Not within the past couple of weeks, at least." She winks.

Shuri sighs. "Well, thanks anyway."

At this, K'Marah huffs. "So much gloom and doom. Shuri, we've been to *one* place and spoken to *one* person. Surely an amazing scientist such as yourself has heard of a disproven theory and subsequent need of a new hypothesis . . ."

Shuri looks at K'Marah, affronted, yes. But also mildly impressed.

"Well?" the other girl goes on. "Pull your pretty little head out of the toilet and *think*. First idea didn't work. What's the revised one?"

Shuri's eyes narrow of their own accord, and part of her bottom lip finds its way in between her teeth.

"That's her *thinking face*, Ororo Storm," K'Marah whispers.

"Shush."

But K'Marah is right: It *is* her thinking face.

"You know, we've also experienced some vegetation shifts as of late. I don't know the forecast in Wakanda, but these global climate fluctuations have caused quite a bit of instability in *our* organic matter."

Which makes Shuri wonder . . . barring the small copse of dead trees the girls passed on their way out of the forest, Yasha was correct in her assumption that Wakanda doesn't seem too terribly affected by the environmental concerns plaguing other nations in the region. At least when it comes to the *organic* matter.

But we're all inhabiting the same Earth, Shuri thinks. *The only thing that makes Wakanda different is the presence of Vibranium . . .*

Then it clicks: The only plants experiencing problems are the ones infused with, or adjacent to, the bizarre meteoric mineral. Maybe the issue isn't with organic matter . . . but *inorganic*. Could ecological changes be affecting Wakanda's most valuable resource? Mutating it somehow? Is that also why she can't get it to bond with a new fabric for T'Challa's suit?

Shuri smiles as a new theory solidifies.

K'Marah sees and smiles, too. "Attagirl, Princess."

Shuri turns to Storm. "Ororo," she says with renewed enthusiasm, "do you know of anyone with extensive knowledge of celestial elements?"

12

INTEL

Ororo *does* know of someone.

But.

"I hate to be the source of disappointment for a *second* time, Princess Shuri, but I'm not entirely sure I could even *get* to the person I'm thinking of," Ororo says sadly. "He's . . . detained at present."

"Detained . . . ?"

Ororo looks back and forth between the girls and sighs. "Is there something happening in Wakanda, Shuri? I understand your concern for saving your herb, and I want to be of service, but I need to know what I am walking into, and—not to discredit your very valid concerns—whether or not sharing highly confidential information with you is worth the risk."

Now Shuri is nervous.

"What I understand from what your brother shared with me years ago, this herb is a vital component of the Black Panther mantle, yes?"

Shuri nods. "In order to fully become the Black Panther, an individual must ingest the herb. It enhances speed, strength, agility, and kinesthetic sensory processing. Makes a man . . ." *or woman*, she thinks, "into a giant cat while simultaneously augmenting the advanced cognitive capabilities we already possess as members of the *Homo sapiens* species."

"Maybe *I* should eat a leaf or two . . ." K'Marah says.

"You'd die," Shuri replies.

Ororo draws back. "Well, that's a bit harsh."

"Yeah, seriously!" K'Marah says. "I was kidding!"

"Well, I wasn't." Shuri focuses her attention back on Ororo. "Anyone who eats of the herb unworthily won't survive it."

"Huh," Ororo says. "I guess that makes sense. I'm sure it prevents would-be megalomaniacs from finding and eating it and becoming instantly powerful. Not that Wakanda *has* any citizens like that." She grins. "How often does a sitting Black Panther have to take it to maintain its effects?"

"Uhh, as far as we know, only once."

"So . . . and forgive me if this question seems dense," Ororo says (and Shuri knows they're about to head downhill), "but if the Black Panther never has to ingest it again, why the urgency to save it *now*?"

Shuri sighs. *Why are grown-ups so thickheaded sometimes?*

"The ritual Challenge Day is coming. That's the day when—"

"—any number of self-selected opponents can challenge T'Challa to a bout of hand-to-hand combat for the throne. I'm familiar."

"Right. Well, at the current rate, the herb will die out completely on the day of the Challenge. So if T'Challa loses—though I don't believe he will," she adds for good measure, "the *new* king and Black Panther will be nothing more than a regular dude who happened to kick T'Challa's butt. This might be fine *within* Wakanda—provided no one decides to run a coup and overtake the throne by force. But what if forces attack from outside?" Shuri says. "What happens if the enhanced abilities of the Black Panther are needed, but unobtainable?"

"And then there's *you*," K'Marah says, jumping in.

Which makes Shuri's already-racing heart leap up into her skull so she can *hear* just how nervous she is. "What do you mean?"

"I mean, I don't know what *your* future plans are, but *I* certainly hope that you'll one day become queen and Black Panther—*Pantheress*, really." She stretches out a hand to look at her fingernails. "It's the only reason I'm training to become a Dora Milaje. So I can go kick butt with you."

A new light flickers on inside Shuri. "K'Marah, that might be the kindest thing you've ever said to me."

"Well, don't get too excited." K'Marah yawns. "If you don't figure out how to save the herbal thingy, no Pantheress action for *you*. I guess T'Challa can keep being Panther once you're queen since he'll allegedly still have the juice in his veins. But not even he will be able to fight forever."

Ororo sighs again. Her gaze drifts out the window, and Shuri sees a flash of lightning in the distance. Had "Ororo Storm" done that just now? Are random lightning strikes a part of *her* thinking face?

"Okay," she says, turning back to Shuri. "I will tell you this, but understand up front that *I* cannot get you access to this person. But knowing you, I'm sure you'll find a way."

Shuri accidentally kicks K'Marah beneath the table in excitement.

"OW!"

"Sorry!" the princess says.

Ororo shakes her head. "Your brother is going to put a price on my head," she says more to the air than to Shuri. "Steve Rogers will, too, if he finds out I shared this intel with a pair of eighth graders."

K'Marah's eyes go wide and she leans in to whisper to Shuri: "Is she talking about *Captain Americ*—"

"Hush, K'Marah!"

Ororo continues: "There is a man named Dr. Erik Selvig who is an expert in . . . cosmically derived paraphernalia, we'll call it. I would be stunned if he *didn't* know all about Vibranium. I'm almost sure he could give you more information about it than anyone else on Earth could."

Barring my father's murderer . . . The thought pops into Shuri's mind unbidden, and she does her best to shake it away. The one person she would never actively seek out is the man who took her and T'Challa's father away, not only from them, but from every citizen of Wakanda.

"The *access* issue, though, is twofold. One: Everyone believes him to be dead. Which means you can't just ask around for how to get to him. Two: From what

I understand, he's a bit . . . unhinged. Steve—Captain America—saved him for reasons he hasn't disclosed, but know that even if you manage to get to him, there's a chance he won't have anything useful to say."

But Shuri has to try, anyway, doesn't she? "Do you know where this man is being held, Ororo?"

The older woman looks right into Shuri's eyes. There's a steadfastness there that Shuri hopes to one day emulate. "He's in London."

A gasp of delighted surprise escapes the princess's lips. "London?"

Ororo gives her a single nod of confirmation. "Correct."

"YES!" And the princess is on her feet with her fist in the air. "K'Marah, we're going to London!"

"Now just a minute, Shuri," Ororo says, rising to *her* feet. "What I will *not* do is permit you two to leave my care on a wild goose chase in a city where you have no contacts—"

"But we *do* have a contact in London!" Shuri exclaims. "There was an entire Hatut Zeraze base there!"

"*Hatut Zeraze* . . ." K'Marah rolls the phrase around on her tongue. "Dogs of War . . . Wait! The Dogs of War are *real*?" she exclaims. "I thought they were urban legend!"

Which doesn't surprise Shuri in the least. Before T'Challa disbanded the group upon his ascent to the throne, there were members of Wakanda's most elite group of spies (and assassins, though Shuri tries not to think about that part) stationed across the globe. Their existence was kept so tightly under wraps, however, most Wakandans believed the Dogs of War to be little more than modern myth. An unconfirmed watchful eye whispered to keep enemies—and disobedient children— on their toes. "They're technically not active anymore, but they were as real as the beads on your braids," Shuri replies. "Though you're not supposed to know that, so shh!" She shakes a finger at K'Marah, then turns back to Ororo. "I'll just touch base with the contact in London, then we'll be out of your rather glorious hair."

"No," Ororo says.

"No?"

"No. Not to go all 'big sis' on you, but I won't allow you two to leave *this* country until I have spoken with an *adult* at your destination."

"But I—"

At the literal lightning flash of *try-me-if-you-want-to* in Ororo's eyes, Shuri's shoulders slump in surrender.

"Yes, ma'am," she says. "We'll have to return to my transport vessel to make contact, though." Shuri lifts the arm with her Kimoyo bracelet to eye level and taps a bead. The words *No Service* illuminate in an arc above her palm.

K'Marah falls asleep almost as soon as the door of the Jeep is shut, so they ride in silence for the first few minutes of the journey back to the plain where the *Predator* is parked, this time with Ororo sitting "shotgun," as Shuri's heard it called.

But a kilometer or so outside the town proper, the weather-wielding woman rotates in her seat and levels the princess with one of her signature (read: abject terror–inducing) narrowed-eye glares. "Who, exactly, are you planning to contact, *Dada*?"

Shuri feels Ororo's sudden suspicion pass over her like a heat wave.

In truth, the princess is surprised it took her this long to ask. Shuri is certain that Ororo, as T'Challa's first flame, previous pen pal, and present greatest ally, knows more about Wakanda's government and intelligence networks than even *she* does. Surely Ororo Munroe is aware of which Hatut Zeraze were stationed in London—she should know exactly whom Shuri intends to reach out to.

She's even met him. He was still in Wakanda back when Ororo and T'Challa were getting acquainted.

"Well . . ." Shuri says. "Not that T'Challa would approve, but . . ."

Based on Ororo's expression *now*, Shuri would say she's finally caught on.

"You're not serious, Shuri. *Him?* Really? Not only will T'Challa not 'approve,' he'll short-circuit!"

"Which is why we aren't going to tell him," Shuri replies.

Ororo just shakes her head. "I guess on the bright side, if anyone can get you to Dr. Selvig, it's him."

"Right?" Shuri says, her excitement building. "That's what I was thinking. He knows everyone."

They lapse back into quiet, and the air around their moving vehicle seems to crackle.

"Shuri?" Ororo says.

"Yes?"

"I'm coming with you."

MISSION LOG

IT'S A GOOD THING ORORO DECIDED TO ACCOMPANY US: IN MY EXCITEMENT ABOUT HAVING A CLEAR PATH TO THE NEXT LEAD, I NEGLECTED TO CONSIDER THE GREAT DISTANCE BETWEEN HAIPO AND LONDON, AND THE TIME IT WOULD TAKE TO MAKE THE JOURNEY.

At top speed, the *Predator* (and fine: The name has grown on me) should've been able to cover the 7,237-kilometer distance in just under three hours. But since I didn't get an opportunity to *test* "flight at that speed with this precise amount of weight," as Ororo put it, we're flying at 75 percent of the maximum velocity, and with the time change, will arrive ninety-three minutes before sunset.

Which means there's a good chance we'll be staying overnight.

And losing more time.

T'Challa didn't blow a gasket and decide to send our entire, Air Force after me like I expected him to, and he *did* agree to stay mum about our little trek and cover for us so Mother won't come after me, either. If I had to guess, I'd say it's because Ororo was standing beside me, smiling and batting her silvery eyelashes, when I made the call.

I told him about the outpost K'Marah and I saw as we left—though he didn't seem too concerned or alarmed. Not entirely sure what to think of that, but at any rate, our contact is expecting us and has been briefed on the purpose of our visit.

All that to say: Everything is in order, and I should be able to recline in my impeccably ergonomically designed, shock-absorbent captain's chair and enjoy our smooth, invisible flight . . .

But I can't. The Challenge is in just over two days, and with each minute that ticks by, my wariness grows.

Something odd: When we returned to the *Predator*—which had been in Invisi-mode the entire time it sat on the plain just outside Haipo—there was a new security image. It was the same sunglasses and kufi-wearing man as before, but in this image, he didn't seem to be looking *up* as much as straight ahead—right into the camera. What's more, it seems this new photo was captured at a much closer distance than the previous one.

I'm not entirely sure what to make of it. I've checked both the software and the security mechanism itself to see if there might be a glitch that would result in the delayed processing or delivery of a captured image, but all appeared to be in working order. It's possible that there was a network issue in flight that deferred the upload . . .

Or there's someone who can, not only see the vessel while it's "invisible," but also managed to follow us to Kenya. (Which is totally and completely improbable. Isn't it?)

Trying not to think *too* much about it. Especially with so many other moving parts.

So. New objectives:

- Get to the White Wolf.
- Get the White Wolf to get me to
  Dr. Selvig.
- Very quickly gather all the very
  helpful information Dr. Selvig
  has stored away in his brain just
  waiting to be set free.
- Return Ororo to Haipo and get back
  to Wakanda as quickly as possible
  (without her being all *Safety
  first!* I think we'll be able to
  fly at closer to 90 percent of
  maximum velocity).
- Save the herb, and by extension,
  the country.

Because this is the way things *have*
to go.
There are no other options.

Oh! A note: Ororo's X-(Wo)Man stretchy—and
moisture-wicking—Storm suit is made of
something called polyelastane. I shall
begin Vibranium-infusion trials as soon as
I manage to acquire a bolt of the fabric.

13

WHITE WOLF

Shuri is just dozing off when the alarm begins to blare. She bolts upright and a sharp pain shoots across the center of her back—might need to reexamine the "impeccable" ergonomics of her captain's chair—but it's nothing compared to the ringing in her ears.

"What is it?" K'Marah shouts, also jolted from her sleep by the shrieking noise. "What's happening?"

"I'm . . . I'm not sure," the princess replies.

What she *is* sure of? She must stay calm.

Thoughts of Baba and predawn mornings spent "meditating" (read: wriggling at his side while *he* meditated) fill her head. "You must maintain your center at all times, child," he used to say in a voice that rang like the deeply resonant music of an upright bass. "Tether yourself to that which is unshakable: the glory and endurance of our great nation."

Shuri takes a steadying breath and attempts to do just that when her Kimoyo bracelet and card begin to vibrate almost simultaneously.

Mother on one, and T'Challa on the other.

A glance around at the cockpit meters and gauges reveals consistent altitude and air pressure within the cabin, and it hits her: The alarm she's hearing is the one she connected to her homeland's nationwide emergency alert system.

Something terrible is happening in Wakanda.

"Oh no," she hears K'Marah say behind her. "Grandmother is calling . . ."

"I think there's something going on back home—"

"SHURI, WHERE ARE YOU?" A hologram of Queen Ramonda leaps up from Shuri's now-illuminated Kimoyo card, and the princess stumbles back. "Mother! I—"

But there's a thump and shout, and the queen gasps and turns to look at something on her right that Shuri can't see before the Kimoyo call drops and her likeness vanishes.

"Mother!" Shuri grabs for the device, but then—

"Sist—you must retur—"

"T'Challa!" Shuri scrambles over to the vessel's radio, thankful she took Ororo's advice and gave him the frequency information when they last spoke, "in case of an emergency that requires the use of more *vintage* technology." "T'Challa, what's going on?"

"—breach at the wester—"

But he keeps breaking up. "Brother?"

"—vasion! Enter at the northea—"

There's a burst of static, and he cuts out entirely.

"T'Challa? T'Challa!"

"Can we turn the alarm *off*?" K'Marah has appeared at Shuri's shoulder with her hands over her ears. "I can't hear myself think!"

"Where is Ororo?" Shuri asks, squatting down to disconnect the alarm sensor from the *Predator*'s speaker system. "We need to reroute."

The interior of the cabin goes suddenly silent, and when Shuri looks up, K'Marah is gazing down at her friend with her head cocked and mouth turned down. "Who?" she says.

"Ororo Munroe, aka *Storm*, aka Mistress of the Elements, aka your personal heroine? Where is she?"

"I have no idea what you're talking about, Shuri."

"This isn't the time for *jokes*, K'Marah," Shuri says, pushing past her friend. "Our country is being *invaded*, and we need to get back to it. Ororo?" she shouts, knocking on the small lavatory door. "Are you in there?"

"There is no Ororo here, Shuri," says a voice from where K'Marah was standing . . .

But it no longer sounds like K'Marah.

Shuri's pulse roars in her ears as blood rushes to her head.

Because she *knows* that voice.

She shuts her eyes and inhales deeply to steady herself—and then she turns.

The woman from her vision is standing between the chairs in the *Predator*'s open cockpit.

"There is no one here to save you, Princess." Puffs of dust leave the woman's mouth with each word, and when she smiles, the cracks in her skin deepen, and a few desiccated chunks drop from her face. "There is no one here to save *you*, and *you* failed to save your country—"

"NO!" Shuri surges toward her, but the woman shoves a hand forward, and the princess is thrown back against the far wall by a grit-filled wind that scorches her skin.

She cries out in pain and tries to get back on her feet.

Another wind hits her, and she inhales what feels like little pieces of burning coal. She coughs. Gags.

"Shuri—"

"*Khusela, khusela . . .*" The voices from the fire ring through Shuri's mind.

The woman is standing over her now. She doesn't want to give up, but what choice does she have? A fissured hand reaches toward her face, but to her surprise, the touch against her cheek is blissfully cool. Her eyelids begin to droop.

"*Shuri . . .*"

"No . . ." The princess whispers, sinking farther into the heat surrounding her. Everything burns. Except for her cheek . . .

"*SHURI! DADA!*"

"No . . ." The faintest whisper now.

"Shuri, you must wake!"

There's a booming crack of thunder, and Shuri sits up.

"Are you okay, sweetheart?" Ororo says, placing a cool hand on her face. "You're very warm."

Shuri stares into Ororo's blue eyes—searching for a tether—but doesn't speak.

"You were having a dream," Ororo continues. "A bad one from the looks of it. Are you all right?"

A dream.

Before she realizes it's coming, Shuri's cheeks are warm and wet.

"Oh dear." Ororo kneels before the princess and takes her hands. She opens her mouth to speak but then . . . just smiles. "You know, this is exactly what your brother was doing when I met *him*."

The stories float to the front of Shuri's mind. T'Challa claims *he* saved *Ororo* from being kidnapped by a white man on a rainy night in the jungle, but Ororo claims *she* saved *T'Challa* from being kidnapped by a group of white men on a Kenyan plain beneath a clear, blue sky.

She peeks over her shoulder. K'Marah, still not feeling well, is curled up beneath one of the Vibranium core–weighted blankets Shuri created for those nights when she couldn't get her brain to stop spinning. With the gentle weight and the sound absorption, she'd sleep like a newborn underneath it—sort of like her friend is doing now.

Should Shuri tell Ororo about the vision at the bonfire? About the nightmare she just had? The weather goddess *is* probably Wakanda's greatest ally out in the wider world.

"I—" Shuri begins, but then there's a ringing noise from just above the radar. *"Warning: This vessel has been detected."*

And back to reality. "Are we not in Invisi-mode?" Shuri says, leaping to her feet to check the flight instruments. They're flying over the English Channel, still a hundred and seventy kilometers or so south of London . . .

The cloaking mechanism is turned up to 100 percent.

Shuri huffs and shakes her head. "There must be a glitch. I tested the stealth tech numerous times, including multiple trips over the marketplace at peak hours, and even a veritable *spy* excursion when I followed T'Challa on one of his surveillance runs around the borders. At no point was I 'detected'—"

Letters and numbers begin to appear on the screen of the *Predator*'s GPS. "What th—"

But then Shuri *and* Ororo are thrown sideways as the aircraft suddenly course corrects.

"Shuri!" Ororo says, trying to prevent the princess from falling. They both collide with the side wall.

"I'm not sure what's happening," Shuri says, doing her best to stay calm. She looks at the aircraft control panel. "How is—"

"*Sorry to intrude.*" A gruff male voice fills the air from the staticky radio.

Which just reminds her of that stupid dream.

"Is everything all right?" K'Marah suddenly says from the back.

Shuri and Ororo both turn to her, and then to each other.

"Wellll . . ." the princess says.

K'Marah, of course, notices their trepidation. "Oh no. Are we losing altitude and on course to crash into the sea in an explosion of watery glory?"

"This aircraft will be remotely directed to a secure location," the staticky voice goes on. "Any attempts to interfere and/or regain control of the vessel will result in immediate engine failure—"

No one on board breathes as what sounds like a scuffle ensues on the other end of the radio. Voices—at least two, and both gravelly and masculine—cut in and out, but Shuri picks up on little blips like "*idiot . . .*" and "*scare the . . .*" and "*protocol*" and "*gimme that . . .*"

Then a voice Shuri *does* recognize (Ororo recognizes it, too, if the roll of her eyes is any indication) crackles through the small speaker: "*Baby sis? That you? We can't see or hear your approach, but there's an odd winged cat–shaped mass of Vibranium crossing into UK airspace from the south . . .*"

Now Shuri smiles and exhales. Of course a group of Wakandans would have the tools and technology to detect Vibranium in the atmosphere, even twenty-eight thousand feet up.

"'Baby sis'?" K'Marah looks more baffled than if someone had told her the Dora Milaje will now be run by men.

"Oh brother," Ororo says, staring at the radio speaker and shaking her head.

Brother, indeed. "K'Marah, you're about to meet my adopted big bro, Hunter."

"Hunter?" K'Marah says.

"I can't believe I'm letting you do this," from Ororo.

"Yes, Hunter," Shuri continues, ignoring Ororo. "Formerly known as the White Wolf."

14
SPACE CADET

In its descent, the *Predator* passes over the bustling city of London, and the girls marvel as Ororo points out things they've only ever read about in their digital European history textbooks: the River Thames and Tower Bridge and Westminster Abbey and Buckingham Palace. There's even a building shaped like a space capsule and what appears to be a giant Ferris wheel—the *London Eye*, Ororo says it's called.

After another three or four minutes, the vessel approaches what appears to be the warehouse portion of an industrial district, and they slow to a near-stop above a cluster of nondescript brick buildings.

Shuri glances at the control panel right as the *Predator* switches into hover mode.

"Whoa!" K'Marah says from her post next to one of the vessel's one-way glass side windows. "Shuri, come look!"

The girls watch in stunned silence as the roof of a building to their right splits down the center and slides open, revealing a landing pad with a white target painted at its center.

The radio crackles again, just about scaring both girls—*and* Ororo—out of their skins. "Seat belts!" Hunter's voice says. "It's windy down here. Landing might be a little turbulent."

And turbulent it is. In fact, by the time they touch down within the building and the roof begins to slide shut above them, Shuri is so nauseated, she can barely move.

She hears the vessel's belly hatch yawn open, and the rhythmic *thu-thunk* of thick heels as someone comes on board. Then a woman she's never seen before appears over her right shoulder. She has something shiny and black draped over her forearm, and is carrying a silver tray topped with three half-filled glasses of bubbly brown liquid. "Princess Shuri," she says with a reverent nod of her head and slight bow. "Honored to have you with us. The polyelastane you requested." She lifts her elbow slightly and gestures with her head to the length of what Shuri realizes is fabric.

The princess slides it off her arm. "Thank you," she says as she takes the woman in. She has beautiful umber skin and an angular face, with extremely close-cropped blond hair. And she's wearing an olive-colored jumpsuit—lots of pockets—and brown lace-up boots.

As Shuri's eyes trail back up the woman's tall frame, they stick on a patch sewn onto her left shoulder: three horizontal stripes, green at the top and bottom, red in the middle, with a centralized image of a red panther against a black circle.

The flag of Wakanda.

"I am Lena," the woman says. "I will be the point of contact for the duration of your stay in London." She hands each of them a glass. "Drink up."

"What is it?" K'Marah says warily, her Dora training actually kicking into gear for once.

It makes Lena smile. "Ginger ale. To settle your stomachs. I wanted to fly you *around* that pocket of bumpy air, but Hunter insisted we pull you through it." She leans forward conspiratorially and lowers her voice. "Feel free to thank him by vomiting on his alligator shoes."

Within minutes, Lena is collecting their empty glasses—the beverage did, in fact, help *easy the queasy*, as K'Marah so aptly puts it—and then they're following her out the aircraft and toward a wide steel door Shuri wouldn't have noticed had she not been looking right at it. As they advance, an iris scanner folds down from the wall, and Lena leans in. "I have heard much of your brilliance, Princess, so you'll have to excuse our humble base of operations," she says as a purple laser, not unlike the one on Shuri's palm scanner, flashes over her eyeball. "Our faction's shift from offensive to observational has . . . taken some getting used to."

Ororo snorts. "I bet."

"At any rate, Hunter is excited to see you." The door opens, and the pair of girls and pair of women step through.

While Shuri doesn't know all the details of Hatut Zeraze's disbandment, she does know that the secret police was created by her father during his reign as king. He'd appointed his adopted son, Hunter, as the leader.

Shuri also knows T'Challa decommissioned the Hatut Zeraze shortly after ascending to the throne . . . and that he and Hunter have never really gotten along.

Years prior to T'Challa's birth, Hunter was taken in by King T'Chaka after a plane crash on Wakandan land killed Hunter's birth family. Shuri suspects that Hunter resents T'Challa for . . . being born, really: As the birth son, it made T'Challa the rightful heir to the Wakandan throne. She also has a hunch that T'Challa, *despite* being the true heir, resented being in Hunter's shadow—she's heard the White Wolf constantly out-performed T'Challa when they were young.

Hunter had left Wakanda on assignment by the time Shuri was born, and she's technically only met him in person twice: first at Baba's funeral, and second at T'Challa's coronation after he bested S'Yan to become king. And she's heard rumors of his brutality.

But he's always been nice to her.

"Second doorway on the left," Lena says, stepping aside so Shuri can walk ahead of her up the bare hallway with dingy tile floors and those terrible fluorescent lights buzzing in the ceiling. "He's waiting for you, so go right in."

The princess's palms dampen as the weight of this impromptu visit settles on her head like a crown of plutonium. What leads will she have if Hunter can't get her to this Selvig fellow? What will she do? All of this time spent getting here and then—

"Well, if it isn't my beautiful baby sister! My, how you've grown!" says the green-eyed man rising from behind a wide desk as Shuri and the others step into the modestly furnished room. He's around T'Challa's height and of a similar build, but bearded and with slick, dark hair that's pulled into a knot on top of his head.

And also: He's . . . not brown.

"*That* is Hunter?" K'Marah says, too stunned to keep her voice down. "But he has the complexion of a *colonizer*!"

Shuri feels her face heat, but the Caucasian man just laughs. "You're very observant," he says with a wink. "Guess you can see why they call me the 'White Wolf.'"

Storm disappears on some intel-acquiring mission for the X-Men, and the princess spends the evening refining the small bit of raw Vibranium she has on board the *Predator* for emergencies, and works at getting it to bind with the polyelastane fabric.

To her great relief, by morning, Hunter has not only managed to locate Dr. Selvig, he also "called in a few favors" (the coldness with which he says the phrase makes Shuri's peace-loving flesh crawl, but she soldiers on) and arranged for Shuri to have ten minutes with him.

And it's a good thing she took K'Marah's "ridiculous" advice and brought her dress: Her cover will involve a brief appearance as a foreign biotechnology student at a benefit gala hosted by the local university where Dr. Selvig is hidden away in an underground laboratory.

"Just be ready to smile and nod," Lena tells her as they move throughout the city making "preparations."

K'Marah, who claims she's been "backhanded by a wave of nausea-inducing jet lag or something," hangs back at the outpost while Lena takes Shuri to a Ghanaian spa in the city to be scrubbed and polished, and with as much as the princess has on her mind, the day blurs by. One minute, she's trying not to squirm while a woman scrubs her feet, and the next, she's back at the outpost— hair, nails, and makeup done (she can wipe off the face but is fully aware that Mother will ask questions about the mani-pedi) and smelling of amber, iris, and patchouli—with Lena helping her into her dress.

Speaking of Lena, she and the two Wakandan men who will accompany them to meet Hunter are all wearing sleek black tuxedos. They're also traveling in a large luxury vehicle she heard someone refer to by the name of another cat of prey: the jaguar.

She hates to admit it considering the circumstances, but for the first time in her life, the princess of Wakanda feels quite fancy. Less a dolled-up bauble made to hang at the queen's side, and more glamorous and important in her own right. The feeling fuels her: Surely T'Challa gets to feel this way all the time.

Stepping into the gala space is jarring: The princess has never seen so many pale-skinned people in one place. With everyone in their fancy clothes, it's like moving through a sea of colored, crystal-studded snow.

Shuri doesn't know the backstory details that have spread about her, but as she crosses the room to meet Hunter in a side hallway as planned, more than a few people stop her to make strange comments about how "impressed" they are that a girl "like *you*" or "where *you're* from" has been "able to accomplish so much." One older Caucasian couple holds her fast for three solid minutes to discuss how "glad" they are she "made it out of the bastion of corruption and poverty that is sub-Saharan Africa."

Shuri finally escapes the crowd, and as she and Hunter take one hallway and staircase after another, her mind spins through the bizarre experience. It's clear that many of the gala attendees hold similar ideas, not only about whatever country she's supposedly from, but about the entire continent. Which seems . . . silly to the princess. What would *these* people think if they knew about Wakanda? Would they even believe it to be real?

Shuri's never been so relieved to exit a too-bright space and step into a darker one.

Because Dr. Erik Selvig's lab is just that: dark.

"We must keep the light low so they don't think we have the cube," he says nonsensically as Shuri and Hunter enter the room. A balding white man in full lab regalia—black slacks, button-down, tie, white coat—scurries around the bizarrely furnished room. There are strange machines scattered about, each with random-looking buttons and dials, the likes of which Shuri has never seen. He bounces between them muttering what sounds to the princess like gibberish under his breath: something about a red skull and a "hydra" and "Kobik." The only thing Shuri *does* recognize is the name "Captain America."

"Dr. Selvig, you have a guest," says the squirrelly man who escorted them through a series of high-security doors to reach the lab.

"A guest?" Selvig replies, startled. "Did they bring the cube? I don't want the cube." And he puts his hands up in surrender before beginning to mumble and pace again.

Shuri jumps right in: "Sir, do you know anything about Vibranium?"

"Which type?" the man says without missing a beat.

At this, Shuri turns to Hunter, not sure she heard the man correctly. Hunter just shrugs.

"There is only one type, sir—"

"Incorrect."

"Huh?"

"There are two known types of Vibranium: Antarctic, the location of which is self-explanatory, and Wakandan, found only in the insular East African nation known as the Wakandas."

The princess tries not to take offense at the word *insular*.

She also wonders if there really is a supply of Vibranium in Antarctica. The notion seems absurd based on what she's been taught her whole life: Vibranium was a gift from Bast and Wakanda is the only nation on Earth with access to it.

But a lot of what she thought she knew has been upended—it's why she's here. Really, is it that far-fetched an idea?

She sets it on a back burner for now. "I mean the type found in Wakanda—"

"Is that where you're from?" The scientist whips around, and Shuri takes a step backward despite there already being a significant amount of distance between them.

She decides to ignore the question—just in case. "Say there was a plant whose cells became infused with Wakandan Vibranium."

His eyes narrow as his gaze shifts to a point somewhere above Shuri's head. "It is feasible, yes."

"Based on what *you* know of Wakandan Vibranium, would a change in the climate or the soil cause that plant to die?"

"Has the plant been moved?" He returns to one of his machines and fiddles with a few dials.

"No, sir," Shuri replies.

"Then no. I have studied both forms of Vibranium—there is an amount of the Wakandan variety in Captain America's shield, in fact—and nothing organic in the earthly sense could disintegrate Vibranium bonds with any other cells. Additionally, the Vibranium itself would cause the plant to be highly adaptable to changes in climate and natural shifts in soil pH," he says.

Shuri deflates. "Okay," she says, trying to keep her voice level. "So what could cause Vibranium-infused organic matter to shrivel and die?"

Now he turns to her and smiles. Which makes her want to leap from her own skin. "Well, Princess," he says, and Hunter steps forward.

"Watch it, old man."

How does he know who I am? Shuri thinks.

Selvig waves the brutish man off and rotates on a heel to begin pacing again. "The only thing that could disrupt Vibranium bonds with organic matter—like plant cells—would be a foreign agent. A poison—"

"But I checked the cells—"

He holds up a hand and Shuri's mouth snaps shut. "A *poison* in the sense of a substance that causes illness or death in living organisms, but one not typically found in nature," he goes on. "Which would mean one of two things." He stops moving and stands up straight with his hands behind his back. "Has there been any abnormal celestial activity over the Wakandas as of late?"

"I don't think so," Shuri says.

"Correct!" Selvig's finger shoots into the air. "The most recent celestial disturbance was over the city of Chicago two nights ago, in fact."

This guy is so weird, Shuri thinks. "Okay . . ."

"So there's your answer. You may go."

Baffled, the princess actually looks around. "Huh?"

"You're dealing with a *mutated* substance." He whips around and looks at her like *Duh, you dummy.*

"Uhhh . . . all right. So this substance is undetectable at the molecular level?"

"None of that matters," he says before his eyes alight on an instrument to Shuri and Hunter's right. He races over to check it. "Your plants aren't dying naturally, and you need to change your question. It's not *what* is killing them. It's *who*."

15

DETECTED

Shuri's mind is reeling as she and Hunter ascend what feel like eight billion steps to get back to ground level from Dr. Selvig's laboratory. Hunter's contact—the squirrelly guy who flinches every time the White Wolf *blinks* in his direction—leads them down a hall away from the festivities in the grand ballroom, and soon the cool night air is hitting Shuri's face.

Could what Dr. Selvig suggested be true? Is there someone *inside* Wakanda deliberately poisoning the heart-shaped herb? Shuri hates to admit it, but the whole way up from the lab, all she could think about was Ororo. Not because the princess thinks *she's* poisoning the herb . . . but because "who" and "mutated" make Shuri think of mutants. (*Is that discrimination?* she wonders.)

Are there any mutants inside Wakanda? That would make them Wakandan mutants. The thought of which is jarring, but . . . well, why wouldn't there be?

But also: Why would a Wakandan want to kill the heart-shaped herb?

The princess is silent for the entire drive back to the outpost, and though she catches Lena eyeing her with concern more than once, Shuri is thankful when the woman doesn't ask any questions.

A call comes in mere minutes before they reach their destination, and it's clear from the wary looks and hushed exchange of whispers that the trio of Wakandan (former?) secret agents is being called to a mission that doesn't involve babysitting a pair of tween rogues.

Once they've pulled the car into an underground garage at the back of the building, Lena turns to Shuri. "Princess, we must attend to some business in the city, but you and your travel companions will be safe here. I will escort you upstairs—"

"That's okay. Just tell me which floor, and you all can go."

Lena opens her mouth—surely to rebut—but then closes it and nods. "Very well, Your Majesty," she says, removing a single bead from her Kimoyo bracelet. "You will need to hold this up to the security scanner within the elevator. Fourth floor. A room has been prepared for you next door to your friend, whom I believe is resting still. You're the third door on the left. Ororo requested quarters with roof access, so she's one floor up at the opposite end of the long hallway."

"Okay. Thank you, Lena." Shuri moves to exit the vehicle.

But Lena's hand lands on her arm. "Are you sure you're all right, Shuri?" she says, face ablaze with what Shuri can only describe as *readiness to throw down*.

It makes the princess feel safer than she has in quite a long while. Which impels her to tell the truth: "To be honest, Lena, I'm not." Shuri turns to her and smiles. "But I will be."

They all watch as Shuri steps into the elevator, and she waves as the doors slide shut.

But she doesn't press the button for the fourth floor. Because right now, Shuri's mind is whirring like a centrifuge, trying to separate what she knows for sure from that which she can only speculate about.

When she gets like this at home, the princess either fidgets with something or takes a long walk. Since it's a delightfully cool night and she doesn't have enough raw Vibranium or the tools she needs to refine it in order to begin the infusion trials on the polyelastane fabric, she chooses the latter, holding the DOORS CLOSE button on the elevator panel for a stretch of a few minutes.

Once she's sure her overseers have had adequate time to not only leave but also return in case something was forgotten, she lets go of the button and stands to the side as the doors reopen. Then she peeks out . . . and releases a head-clearing sigh of relief when she sees that the coast is clear.

She was right about the area they're in: It's full of warehouses and three- to five-story industrial buildings. From the front, she can see that the building they're in—which Hunter let slip is Wakandan-owned—is much larger than she realized. She knew it was five floors high but had no idea it encompassed an entire block.

Which just sets Shuri's brain to spinning again. Where else in the world are there Wakandans stationed? The princess met three emissaries from her homeland in addition to her adopted brother, but with a building this size, there have to be *more* people working here. She wonders how many.

Are there outposts like this in major cities across the globe? Shuri finds the thought staggering—even more so than the notion of T'Challa revealing their existence to everyone. It makes a series of doubts burble in her stomach: There's obviously much more to being a ruler than she realized. Does she even have what it takes?

The past few days flood back over Shuri: from the failed suit trials to the Taifa Ngao and first mention of the word *invasion*. From the bonfire and vision, to the discovery of the dying herbs. From seeing T'Challa and Okoye with the war council to her and K'Marah's bizarre exit from Wakanda. From the overwhelming heat in Kenya to meeting Dr. Selvig.

A breeze rustles some debris just over the edge of the curb, and Shuri realizes how cool it's gotten. Is midsummer in London always this nippy at night?

The princess rubs her skinny arms and picks up speed. What she *should* do is return to the outpost, wake K'Marah, and get them en route back home. She's wasted enough time away: The Challenge is *tomorrow*, and though she hasn't exactly solved any problems, getting some surveillance set up both in the field and in that one pocket of the forest seems like the next logical step.

Shuri has just rounded the corner that'll put her at the back of the building when a figure steps out of an alley just ahead of her, but on the opposite side of the street. A man, she believes. Tall and thin and wearing an open tan trench coat with the high collar flipped up against the bite in the air. And though his sudden presence sends a very much *non-temperature-related* chill skittering from the top of Shuri's still perfectly styled head to the tips of her polished toes, she keeps her eyes forward. Pretends he's not there.

But then he crosses to her side.

And heads right in her direction.

"Don't panic," she says under her breath. Why had she thought it a good idea to roam a place she's never been, at night and alone?

As the distance between them shortens, she makes the decision to nod in greeting and keep it moving.

Five meters and closing fast (*sheesh*, this guy has long legs).

Three.

One—

"Good evening, Princess Shuri," he says in passing.

"Good eveni—"

Wait.

Shuri stops dead. And now can't breathe. Because she can see his shadow. And she knows that, whoever he is, he's coming around to face her.

She can't move. Not when the man stands at his full height in front of her. Not when she notices his charcoal-colored kufi and his dark sunglasses, or when he slowly reaches up to fold down his collar and she sees his ashen hands. Not even when he removes the sunglasses and she sees the bloodshot eyes and the cracked skin of his face. It's not nearly as pronounced as the woman in her vision/dream, but close enough for Shuri to have zero doubt that the man from the *Predator*'s security photos and the Wakanda-crushing woman are connected.

"Such a pleasure to make your acquaintance," he says in a deep rasp with a mocking bow of his head.

"You've been following us. Since we flew over you near the border. You can see my aircraft."

"Not exactly, no," he replies, clasping his hands in front of him. "But I have known precisely where you were during every minute of your journey."

But how?

Shuri's wheels spin, desperately seeking a viable course of action. She could run, but she knows he's likely to catch her. There are also no guarantees that he's alone.

The next option is an attempt to fight . . . though she hasn't trained in over a year—*thanks, Mother*—and swift movement will be difficult in this blasted dress. She wants to kick *herself* for wearing it.

"Who are you?" she asks, a feeble effort to keep him talking, though she has no idea what that will accomplish. Perhaps her trio of former Dogs of War will happen to turn the corner at just the right moment to come to her rescue.

"*Who* I am is of no consequence, Princess. The only thing that *truly* matters is what I plan to do."

"And what's that?" Shuri carefully, clandestinely shifts her feet into a fighting stance. Because she has a hunch about what his response will be.

"Well, to start, I intend to prevent your return to your beloved homeland." And with that, his hand shoots out quick as a flash, reaching for Shuri's throat.

16

A PANTHER
AND HER DORA

Shuri feels something like fire surge through her veins, and a lightning reel of recollections featuring T'Challa—of her days sparring and training—sparks through her mind quicker than a blink, igniting her muscle memory.

She uses her much shorter height to her advantage: ducking so that the man's hand closes around air, and then surging forward to plunge her bony shoulder into his unguarded midsection.

He stumbles backward, but with his unnaturally long arms is able to get a grip on Shuri's bicep as she tries to pull away. "Gotcha—"

The princess's left foot collides with his mouth as she twists beneath his arms and kicks her leg up behind her—*riiiiiiip!* goes the dress (oops)—escaping his grasp in the process.

As he folds at the waist, and his hands instinctively rise to his face, Shuri stands up fast, catching the underside of his chin with the thickest part of her skull to knock his head back, and then completing the blow with a full-force kick to his sternum.

He falls this time.

Shuri turns as fast as she can and attempts to make a run for it—

But the man manages to pin a piece of her ripped and dragging dress to the concrete with his foot.

She goes down hard, biting her tongue as her chin hits the pavement.

"Shuri . . ." she thinks she hears in a tinny, distant voice, but she must be imagining it. Her ears are ringing, and it takes a few seconds too long for her head and vision to clear: She's forcefully flipped from her stomach to her back and finds the man standing over her, lip busted and rage flickering in his dark pupils with every labored breath.

"You will regret your actions," he says. And he stretches down and grips the front of her dress in his fist to pull her to her feet . . .

But then one of his knees buckles, and he turns to look behind him.

Which gives Shuri just enough time to slip from his grasp and reverse roll to her feet.

She's upright just in time to see her rescuer land a roundhouse kick to the guy's jaw.

K'Marah.

A string of bloody drool flies from kufi-man's mouth as his head whips right.

"Eww!" the princess says.

It's the wrong move. He locks her in his livid gaze as he regains his balance, then lunges for her with hands outstretched.

Shuri yelps and manages to dodge so his grasping fingers close around air, but her feet tangle in her stupid, ragged-edged dress. Down she goes again, and this time, he doesn't waste a single moment. Her mouth opens, ready to scream, as he reaches to yank her to her feet—

But then his eyes go wide and surprised before they roll up in his head, and he collapses to the side with a thud.

Once he's out of the way, Shuri can see K'Marah

standing with both hands wrapped around what she recognizes as the thick, black marble panther figurine that was perched on the bookcase in Hunter's office. The mini-Dora's chest is heaving.

"Did he hurt you?" she says as she sets the stone cat aside to help pull Shuri to her feet. "Oh no, your chin!"

"I'm fine, I'm fine," the princess replies. "Thank you for coming to my rescue. Now let's tie him up before he comes to so he can't get away. Whoa . . ." She tries to stand up on her own, and her head swims.

"Cool it, sister," K'Marah says. "Here, you lean against the wall, and *I* will tie him up, *capisce*?"

"Ca-*what*?" Shuri replies, letting her head drop back against the brick.

"Ah, it's an old expression I learned from mid-twentieth-century white-American gangster movies."

"Of course you watch those," Shuri says with a roll of her eyes.

As K'Marah secures the man's hands and feet, woefully using strips of fabric from Shuri's ruined dress, Shuri uses her Kimoyo bracelet to call and let Hunter know the location of the trespasser. After a quick search of his pockets and person for evidence, weapons, etc. (they find nothing), K'Marah blindfolds him and ties a strip of fabric around his mouth as Hunter instructs. "You better be glad I didn't have my spear, you jerk!" she shouts into his unconscious face as she does so. Then the girls drag him into the shadows, leaving him there to be collected by Hunter's crew, before they scurry down the remainder of the block to the back entrance of the building as fast as their small feet will carry them.

Which isn't very fast. And both girls notice. "You *sure* you're not hurt?" K'Marah asks just as Shuri says, "You're not looking too hot . . ." They laugh, but Shuri knows it's more to break the tension than because something is funny.

"How'd you know I was in trouble?" Shuri can't help but ask once they're back in the parking garage, waiting for the elevator.

"I think you accidentally Kimoyo-called me." K'Marah lifts Shuri's wrist and holds it up to her own so they can both see the pair of illuminated beads. "I could hear the . . . scuffle. So I grabbed the first heavy thing I could find—and carry—and used our connected call to track you."

Track her. Hmm.

The elevator *dings*, and the girls step on the second the doors begin to slide open. As they ascend through the building, the weight of what just happened settles down around them. Shuri is *certain* there are a million-and-one questions lining up single-file on her friend's tongue, most of which she won't be able to answer. She braces herself as she hears the little intake of breath that lets her know K'Marah is about to speak.

But the other girl says only one word: "Tomorrow."

After getting cleaned up and changed, the girls decide—well, Shuri decides *for* them—that they'll sleep inside the *Predator* for the sake of making a swift exit as soon as they awaken. K'Marah replaces Hunter's panther figurine, and Shuri leaves a note on his desk to thank him and the others for their help and hospitality. Then utilizing the bead Lena gave her, which, as Shuri suspects, is akin to a master key for every high-security lock in the building, the girls retrace their steps to the landing pad—thanks entirely to K'Marah's flawless, Dora Milaje–trained sense of direction.

K'Marah, who really *wasn't* looking too hot, especially after the adrenaline subsided, is out like a pinched candlewick the moment she pulls the Vibranium blanket up over her shoulders and proclaims, "This blanket is the *best*." (Shuri knows it's going to disappear as soon as they arrive home.)

But try as Shuri might—even with her own delightful blanket—she is unable to sleep. And it's not even what she *knows* or has recently experienced that keeps her eyes wide and mind reeling. It's what she *doesn't* know: how the dry-skinned man has been keeping tabs on them.

With a huff, she climbs down from her bunk and goes to the *Predator*'s control panel, powering up both the electrical and navigation systems. While she knows that her Wakandan cohorts here in London surely have the technology to detect a flying object—including a soundless, invisible one with its radar turned off—she *must* figure out how kufi-man detected them on their way out of Wakanda.

Shuri programmed the detection alert mechanism to go off when one of two things happens: either something interacts with the *Predator*'s GPS signal, or it's physically spotted in flight—the latter of which is determined by tiny cameras all over the mirroring panels that track the focus of the eye, and can therefore "tell" when the vessel has been spotted.

Based on the security images, Shuri knows the latter set off the alarm just after they crossed the border.

But she's also fairly certain the man said he *couldn't* see the aircraft. ("Not exactly, no.") Is there a reason for him to have lied?

After running an overall avionics scan for glitches or bugs (there are none), Shuri scrolls through the signal log to trace all of the *Predator*'s digital interactions—with satellites, ground computers, etc. When nothing strange turns up there either, the princess runs an electronic scan of the cabin to see if there's a trackable signal lurking somewhere else on the aircraft.

A yellow dot lights up on the screen, and Shuri gasps.

There *is* a rogue signal.

And it's coming from K'Marah's bunk.

With the assistance of her Kimoyo bracelet and a few taps, the princess is able to reverse engineer the signal-acquiring mechanism in her Kimoyo card, turning it into a tracker-tracker that will pick up on any item that has been traced remotely. Then slowly, quietly, Shuri approaches her sleeping friend, waving the card over her blanketed body like a metal detector.

K'Marah is sleeping on her back with an arm draped across her face. And as soon as Shuri nears her head, the Kimoyo card lights up like a fiery flare.

She moves it closer to the pillow, and it dims. So she brings it back up over K'Marah's cheek. Signal's a bit stronger. Over her mouth, nose, eyes, onto her arm . . . brighter and brighter still until she gets to her wrist.

Which is when the card quietly *pings* and turns green.

K'Marah's fancy bracelet.

Odd.

Shuri carefully unclasps it from her friend's arm and carries it to the front of the *Predator* for examination.

Once there, she holds it up and shines her Kimoyo card flashlight over it. It certainly doesn't *look* out of the ordinary—for K'Marah the Glam, at least. The smoky-colored glass beads are cracked on the inside, which Shuri must admit creates a cool, sparkly-but-not-obnoxious effect. Though where someone would hide a tracking device . . .

She extinguishes the flashlight and sets the Kimoyo card aside. Then lays the bracelet across her palm.

The wave of lethargy that instantly crashes down over her is so intense, Shuri's knees buckle and she has to use the back of her captain's chair to keep from falling.

She forces herself back fully upright, gaze fixed on the unassuming piece of jewelry. Then, mustering strength she didn't realize she'd need, she uses the opposite hand to lift the bracelet so she's holding it in the air by the clasp like before.

Her sense of vitality returns. In fact, for the breadth of a few seconds, Shuri could swear she feels every cell of her body surge with life.

She raises her forearm to eye level and carefully lays the bracelet over her wrist.

Boom. Exhausted. And a bit nauseated this time, too.

She picks it up . . .

And she's back to full force, even more awake and alert and *alive* than before.

Is *this* why K'Marah has been so tired and queasy?

"Wow!" She hears from behind her. "What time is it? Are we about to depart? Where is Queen Goddess Ororo-Storm?"

Shuri quickly stashes the bracelet behind her back as she whips around to face her friend. Her friend . . . who *looks* better. K'Marah's chin is high and her eyes are bright and her skin is glowing.

For a moment, Shuri can only stand and blink and stare.

"Why are you looking at me like that?" K'Marah says with a stretch. "Bast, I needed that rest. This is the most refreshed I've felt since we left home."

And that's all Shuri needs to hear.

"K'Marah," she says, going to sit beside the girl she realizes truly *is* her best friend. She holds the bracelet up, and K'Marah's eyebrows rise with it. "I think it's time we talk."

MISSION LOG

KEEPING THIS ONE SHORT BECAUSE WE NEED TO DEPART, BUT I JUST HAD A CONVERSATION WITH K'MARAH THAT WAS QUITE . . . REVELATORY. IT WENT SOMETHING LIKE THIS:

> Me: Old friend, I'm not sure where you got this bracelet, but it's both being used to track us and make you sick.
>
> Her (staring at it, first in disbelief, and then . . . something else): Oh.
>
> Me: Do you remember where you got it?

Her: (*silence*   *avoidance*
refusal to meet my eyes)

Me: K'Marah . . .

Her (sighing): You won't judge?

Me: Judge what?

Her: If you say "I told you so," I
will never speak to you again.

Me: K'Marah, what are you talking ab—

Her: Henny gave it to me.

Me: (*silence* *avoidance* *refusal
to meet her eyes*)

Her: (*see line above*)

Me: I thought you said you've never
met him in person?

Her (sighing again): I haven't.
I . . . well, I told him I was
going on a trip—

Me: K'MARAH!

Her: I know, I know. For what it's
worth, I didn't mention *you*. But
the package arrived by courier an
hour later.

Me: So . . . he knows where you live, then?

Her: (*silence* *avoidance* *refusal to meet my eyes*) He must've . . . tracked my IP address.

Despite how quickly my mental cup ranneth over with questions—*Did you tell him of your training and career path? Our friendship? Your position as the Mining heiress? Was his goal to track you . . . or me?*—I said no more in the moment.

Because in spite of the questions, other pieces were clicking together in my mind. Like the existence of a (highly probable) relationship between this boy K'Marah thought was a friend, and the grown man who has been using the bracelet the boy gave K'Marah to follow us across two continents.

Though he can follow us no more—Hunter and crew delivered him to a maximum-security cell deep underground in the same building where Dr. Selvig's bizarre laboratory is located—I have the distinct suspicion that man was *not* out for the good of Wakanda.

Which would mean this boy K'Marah was communicating with likely does not have our nation's best interests at heart, either.

I managed to locate the bracelet's tracking mechanism and succeeded in reversing it. Now the next time someone attempts to pinpoint K'Marah's (our?) location, *we* will be alerted to *their* precise whereabouts.

I also succeeded in heating the bracelet beads to a pre-melt point that permitted me to collect a tiny bit of not only the coating but the glass itself. It is presently undergoing molecular analysis, and as soon as we are back in Wakanda, the result will upload to my database of chemical compounds for cross-referencing.

Ororo has just returned, so after I debrief her, we'll be on our way. I have no idea what awaits us back in our homeland and can only assume that T'Challa and Mother's silence is a result of all-consuming Challenge Day preparations.

At least that is my hope.

Any *other* reason no one seems to have noticed I'm gone . . . Well. I'd rather not think about it.

17

PREPARATION

One bright spot on Shuri's horizon: The polyelastane fibers accept a full-strength Vibranium infusion without disintegrating. The turnaround time will be tight, but provided they cross the Wakandan border by zero eight hundred hours and the fabric is waiting outside the entrance to her lab as she requested when she contacted the clothier, she should be able to get it infused and delivered to the clothier in time for him to work his sewing sorcery and have a habit prototype ready just before the Challenge.

Whether or not big bro will consent to wearing it for his ritual showdown is another question, but at least the princess has *something* semi-manageable to ponder over as they make their way back to Wakanda. Everything else might be crumbling, but T'Challa will soon have a moisture-wicking, kinetic energy–absorbing—and *storing* . . . and *expelling*—super-ultra-*STRETCHY* Panther Habit just like he asked for.

(She tries not to think about the fact that the perfect suit for T'Challa won't matter if he's bested.)

They part ways with Ororo three hundred kilometers north of Wakanda, shortly after Shuri begins their initial descent, and she exits the *Predator* with a look of fierce pride. But the closer they get to home, the more anxious the princess feels.

There are just so many unknowns. And the more she attempts to connect the dots, the less they seem connected at all. Ororo suggested Shuri inform T'Challa of the bits she does know, but the princess can't bring herself to do that because what exactly would she tell him? *"I got attacked by a man desperately in need of shea butter—who may be linked to a cracked-skinned* woman *I saw crushing Wakanda in a vision—after he tracked us using a bracelet that was delivered to K'Marah under the guise of being from a boy she met online who is supposedly a Jabari. OH, and I still haven't solved the herb problem, so they'll all be dead soon and you'll just have to stay Black Panther forever so PLEASE DON'T LOSE THE CHALLENGE! Here's a new suit, by the way!"*

It all sounds like nonsense.

And Shuri? Well, she feels like a failure.

Fifty kilometers north of the border, Shuri decreases the *Predator*'s speed and cranks up the rate of descent so that the girls can enter through the forest just like they exited: invisible, untraceable by radar, and utilizing Kimoyo tech to prevent signaling a border breach alarm.

And because she can't resist a peek at the area where they saw that encampment and were first "spotted" by their kufi-capped London assailant, Shuri makes a last-second decision to fly that way.

It's a decision she comes to appreciate . . . and regret.

"Uhhhh, Shuri?" K'Marah says from beside her.

"Yup."

"Not good . . ."

"Mm-hmm."

Because the girls can see that the small encampment a couple of kilometers beyond the Wakandan border with Niganda has grown. It's no longer a gathering of a handful of men with tents and campfires.

Now arrayed beneath them in perfectly formed lines is a certifiable army.

Shuri corrects course, heading northeast so they can cross the border a bit away from the impending invaders. As they cruise along the edge of the forest, Shuri taking full control of the vessel so she can turn at precisely the right angle for entry at a different point, K'Marah, who is standing with her forehead pressed against the front window, suddenly cries out: "Shuri! The forest!"

The princess peeks right and gasps. "Bast be with us . . ."

"Whoa!" K'Marah loses her footing as the *Predator* begins to tilt. "I know it's bad down there, Princess, but don't forget to drive!"

"Oh." Shuri rights the aircraft and tries to keep her breath steady as she faces back forward. But what she just saw is seared into her memory: a swath of dead trees like the ones she saw on the way out, and all around them, nonfunctional mechanized ones, the leaves of which are spotted that sickly yellow.

"It's spreading, Shuri!" K'Marah says, returning to her window post. "I can see it! More of the trees are dying!"

"Hold on tight! I'm turning around!"

Though it's risky flying *over* the greenery—and Shuri knows it will trigger the alarms in the capital—she also knows that a bird's-eye view will allow for the best scan of the trees so she can gather accurate information about how quickly they're being killed/disabled, and in which direction.

"K'Marah?"

The other girl turns.

"If we don't make it out of this alive, thank you for being my friend."

K'Marah rolls her eyes. "Save the drama for your mama, Princess."

It puts a temporary smile on Shuri's face as she accelerates just the slightest bit to push the *Predator* across the tree line and begin the terrain scan.

For a solid two seconds, Shuri thinks they're in the clear. But then the now too familiar alert rings out: *"Warning: This vessel has been detected."*

"Drat," from K'Marah.

"I can think of worse things to say," Shuri counters. "Let's just hope no one starts shooting or tries to overtake our navigation." She thinks of their friends in London. "Again."

The results of the scan pop up. "The security forest is deactivating by combination of organic death and mechanical failure at a rate of zero-point-three meters per second in the direction of the baobab plain. One thousand and sixty-two meters have already succumbed, and whatever is causing this shutdown appears to be creating a path approximately eight meters wide. As there are ten kilometers of forest between the border and the edge of the field, a way straight into Wakanda will be cleared in . . ." She taps around on the screen. "Eight hours, sixteen minutes, and thirty-three-ish seconds."

"Uhhh," is all K'Marah can say.

Not that it matters: Shuri is now clicking and swiping and tapping around on her Kimoyo card. "The Challenge is set to begin in"—*tap-click-swipe*—"eight hours, twenty minutes, and twenty-seven seconds." She shakes her head. "I really hate to admit it, but this was an exquisitely executed invasion plan."

K'Marah snorts.

"Hey, S.H.U.R.I.! Call T'Challa!" Shuri shouts into the air.

"Calling T'Challa," replies the same mechanically pleasant voice who just told them their very *detected* goose is cooked.

"Are you serious?" K'Marah says, flopping down in her seat.

"What? I have to tell him abou—"

"You named your AI after *you*? This is worse than the laboratory greeting!"

"It's an acronym! Stands for Super Heroics Universal Remote Interface . . ."

"Sure, it is—"

A hologram of T'Challa pops up in the center of the control panel. He's shirtless. "Shuri!" he says, clearly out of breath.

"T'Challa! There—"

"Well, *hello*, Your Majesty!" K'Marah says, looking at the hologram a bit more intently than Shuri is expressly comfortable with.

"Oh! Hello, future Dora! I am glad you two are safe—"

"T'Challa, where are you? We must speak to you at once!"

The hologram ducks, bobs, and throws a punch.

"Ooh!" K'Marah says, eyebrows lifting in delight.

The princess gags.

"Shuri, I can't—"

"*PLEASE*, T'Challa! It is urgent!"

"Stop, stop," he says to someone they can't see. Then he looks right at Shuri. "I'm at the Den. And as you've interrupted my training on *this* day, it better be."

When they step into the Den, the large, multistory facility where every warrior in Wakanda—from the border guards to the Dora Milaje—begins their respective training, Shuri gets smacked with a wave of nostalgia.

"Sheesh, I forgot how much it stinks in here," K'Marah says, getting hit with a different wave.

On the main level, where the youngest and newest trainees spend most of their time, there's a boxing ring for sparring, a sand pit for rod work, and a spring floor for acrobatics.

All three flood her with memories of Baba, and the days she was permitted to spend time here. "I miss this place," she says. *I miss him.*

But once they ascend to the third floor—the Special Forces wing—and Shuri sees her brother (with a shirt on now, thank Bast), she's back to business.

"T'Challa, there is an invasion mounting! At the Nigandan bord—"

"I know." And he takes a shockingly nonchalant drink of water.

"You *know*?"

"Of course I do." He walks past her and K'Marah to a table lined with various deadly weapons. Shuri sees three swords, one long and slightly curved, and two short; a variety of differently weighted spears (Shuri remembers him teaching her about the importance of weight); a set of nunchaku; an ax. He picks up a pair of daggers and turns back to face them, raising his arms. "I am the king."

K'Marah looks on the verge of fainting.

(*How vile*, Shuri thinks.)

"They are somehow creating a path in by neutralizing the security forest—"

"I am aware."

"—and they'll be able to break through, *right* at the field, five minutes before the Challenge begins!"

T'Challa sighs. He comes over and puts his hands on Shuri's shoulders and looks her right in the eye. "Shuri," he says. (Shuri tries to keep her breathing even despite the daggers sticking up on each side of her head, but she'll admit that it's difficult.) "Listen to yourself," he goes on. "You have interrupted the *king* of this nation, on the day that others will be permitted to challenge him for the throne and Panther mantle, because you think him unaware of the threat of invasion? At his own borders?"

Shuri gulps. "I—"

"While I can appreciate your zeal, Sister, it is clear that you are often lacking in both reason and foresight. I have known of this invasion threat for weeks now. And I can assure you"—now he smiles—"that it will not succeed. We are well prepared."

But Shuri's not ready to just . . . give up.

Because something still doesn't feel right.

"You are postponing the Challenge, then?" she says.

"Of course not." He moves away from her and into the center of a circle printed on the red rubbery floor. Begins to swoop and dip and jab with the daggers. "We will not shirk tradition for an easily routable threat."

"Well, what about the offensive?" Shuri says, already knowing the answer but unable to stop herself from asking. "Are you sending an army out to take them down?"

"Have they breached our borders, Shuri?"

"Well, no, but—"

"You, of all people, know that 'the offensive' is not our way." He does a spectacular flipping kick—knives in hand—and lands with his back to the princess. Then turns around. "Not that you *should* be privy to this information, but the moment our border is crossed, land and air troops are at the ready to thwart this so-called invasion before it can even begin."

Shuri clenches her fists, incensed. How dare he speak to her as though she knows nothing. As though the safety and security of Wakanda is not also HER highest priority—

Her Kimoyo bracelet buzzes, pulling her back to her senses. So she turns away from T'Challa and taps to reveal the message.

It's an alert from the *Predator*. A couple of Shuri's tests now have results.

Then a second alert pops up. This one even more jarring.

"K'Marah, we need to go," she says to her friend, grabbing her arm and pulling her toward the elevator.

Because while T'Challa might be *sure* the invasion won't be an issue, Shuri's not convinced.

Especially now.

"Molecular match," the first alert said.

Followed closely by *"Signal acquired."*

18

SIGNS AND WONDERS

Shuri blinks.

Rubs her eyes . . . and blinks again.

"K'Marah?" she says to her friend. The girls are standing inside the *Predator*, which is still parked out behind the Den, staring at rotating holograms of identical molecules. "Are you seeing what I'm seeing?"

"If you mean matching ball-stick diagram thingies, then yes," K'Marah replies.

"It's a molecule. A pair of identical ones, in fact."

"I believe you, Princess."

And though the words floating *beneath* the matching molecules are SUBSTANCE UNKNOWN, the one above says MATCH.

And it's the only one that matters.

"K'Marah, *that* molecule," Shuri says, and points to the one on the right, "came from the bracelet you were wearing."

"You mean the one that was more or less sapping my life force?" Her eyes go stormy. "Just *wait* till I use some of your gadgets to pinpoint that idiot boy's home addr—"

"Yes. That bracelet," Shuri says. She takes a deep breath. "What's interesting is that the *other* molecule"—now she points to the one on the left—"was pulled from the roots of a dead heart-shaped herb plant."

"Huh." K'Marah rubs her chin.

"Right."

Shuri sees K'Marah's head cock to one side in her peripheral vision. "So . . . does that mean what I think it means?"

"What do you think it means?"

"That whoever made my—I mean *the*—bracelet is the reason your plants are dying?"

Shuri's eyes narrow. "Likely."

K'Marah snorts. "Figures."

"Huh? What figures?"

"That the first boy I really like would try to mur-der me."

They stand in silence for a few seconds longer, watching the matching molecules turn.

"So would I be right in assuming Henny—*if* that's even his name—has been working for that lanky loser we fought in London?"

"It's possible," Shuri replies. "Or lanky loser could be working for Henny. If that's his name." She pauses. "If it's a him, even."

"You think it's a girl?"

Shuri shrugs as the horrific face of the dry woman floats across her mind. "Could be either. Or neither. Or both. Not ruling anyone out."

K'Marah nods. "I hear that."

"The person is here," Shuri says, flicking her eyes to the GPS screen on the left. There's a blinking red dot at the base of the mountain region.

"Huh?"

"In Wakanda. I flipped the signal-tracing mecha-nism in your bracelet so that the tracker inside works *as* a tracker. When we were in the Den, I got a message that a signal was acquired—which means someone made an attempt to figure out where we are."

"Whoa."

"I'll admit, I wasn't expecting anyone to try to track us again. I figured with our London assailant incapacitated by our Wakandan cohorts, that would be that," Shuri says. "Tweaking the tech was more a . . . cautionary measure. In case we got lucky."

"Are you saying *this* is luck?"

Shuri shrugs again. "At least we have a lead."

"Okay . . . so whoever is looking for us is in the mountains now?"

The princess stares at the blinking dot. "Well, they *were*. The signal was lost."

"Do they know where *we* are?"

"Don't think so," Shuri says. "If I did my job right, they should've gotten an error message instead of a location for us."

"You clever little panther cub."

Shuri smiles. "Thank you."

"So, what now?"

The princess taps her bracelet, and the images disappear. "Have a seat and buckle up," she says, settling into her captain's chair and powering up.

K'Marah complies. "Where are we going?"

"To my lab," Shuri says. "I'll run some more tests and start the Vibranium infusion for T'Challa's new suit."

"Okay."

They rise in hover mode, and then take off.

"Umm, Shuri?"

"Yes, K'Marah?" Shuri wouldn't say it aloud right now, but her chest tightens at the sight of the capital disappearing beneath them. What if the invasion plans succeed?

"Not to be annoying, but then what?"

"Huh?"

"After you do the testing and suit thing?"

"Oh." It is an excellent question. "Well, then we wait."

"For?"

"For your bracelet-gifter to try to track us again."

"A-ha." K'Marah's eyes drop to her hands in her lap. "You really think they will?"

"Absolutely," Shuri says, steel in her voice now. "And when they do? We will find them."

The box of polyelastane fabric is waiting in the cavern hallway outside Shuri's lab door when the girls arrive. And to the princess's delighted surprise, it takes way less time than she anticipates to complete the infusion (such is the beauty of having a massive stash of refined Vibranium lying around). As soon as it's complete, she sends it by drone to the waiting clothier.

Shuri then starts a series of *new* tests on the substance from the bracelet and herb roots—to see its effects on variously sized machines. It turns out there are only trace amounts on the piece of jewelry, so whoever gave it to K'Marah didn't want *her* to die. But Shuri's hunch is that the same unknown substance used to kill the heart-shaped herb is also being used to create the entry path through the security forest for the invading army.

After the mechanical deaths of a spare Kimoyo card, a drone, and a four-wheeler Shuri sometimes used to travel between the palace and the lab—all made with or enhanced by Vibranium—she's fairly certain her hypothesis is correct. Interestingly enough, the substance has no effect on electronics *without* Vibranium, though it does utterly trash any organic matter it touches, including a mango, a black segmented millipede (Bast rest its many-legged soul), and a succulent plant Okoye brought to the princess from some place called California.

And then it happens.

The princess is tinkering with the "CatEyez" (the *z* was K'Marah's idea) just for the sake of killing time when her Kimoyo card buzzes like an angry wasp. "Ahh!" she jumps, not only dropping the tiny screwdriver she was using, but also bumping the edge of the lab table so hard, her entire tool kit goes crashing to the floor.

"Typical," K'Marah says from behind her.

"You know what—"

"Signal acquired," the computerized voice says with zero enthusiasm.

The girls look at each other . . . and both lunge toward the device.

"What's it say?" K'Marah asks, peeking over Shuri's shoulder.

Shuri stares at the red dot, now solid instead of flashing because the tracker is actively in use.

A spark of fury ignites inside her as the dot moves. "I should've known."

"What? Where is he? She—" K'Marah blows out a frustrated breath. "Where are they?"

"Close by. And moving through a different part of the forest," Shuri replies.

She looks at K'Marah. "They're headed to the Sacred Field."

19

HENBANE

After tucking two pairs of CatEyez into her knapsack, and grabbing a few of the "gentler weapon" prototypes—ones that disarm and disable, but don't destroy—from her arsenal, the princess and her mini Dora Milaje get on their way. It's a short journey to the field, and the little tracker-tracking light on Shuri's Kimoyo card screen stays solid through the duration of their trek.

Whoever is behind the bracelet, at least, is *definitely* in the field.

It's clear something is wrong as the girls stealthily

approach the concealed entrance: There's no one manning it.

Typically, Kufihli or one of the other priests would be standing guard on the other side to prevent intruders—wild animals, wandering children, or wannabe Black Panthers—from waltzing in.

But that's precisely what Shuri and K'Marah do.

It's dead quiet—no pun intended—and dark inside the cave-like space due to the lack of the herb's soft phosphorescence. Shuri didn't realize *how* incandescent the plants naturally are until just now. The lack of light is disorienting, especially since they can't utilize any other sources of illumination without giving themselves away.

But then she remembers—

"K'Marah," she whispers, "there are two pairs of those glasses I showed you down in the bag. Put one on and give me the other."

K'Marah does just that. "I . . . still can't see anything."

"Tap the right side and say 'scotopic-mode.'"

K'Marah complies, but as Shuri does the same and the area around them goes purple and bright through the lenses, she can see K'Marah shaking her head. "Of course she couldn't just call it *night vision*," K'Marah grumbles.

But then the shorter girl turns her head and—

"Shuri!" she whispers furiously, pointing to something in front of them and to the right. "Look!"

As Shuri's eyes slowly adjust, she can see a series of large lumps come into focus.

"Are they . . . dead, do you think?" K'Marah asks.

And that's when it crystallizes: The haphazardly distributed shapes are the collapsed—and hopefully just *unconscious*—forms of Kufihli and three of the priestesses.

"Shuri!" K'Marah hisses, more urgently this time.

"Wha—"

But Shuri sees *exactly* what. Back in the far-left corner of the field, some hundred meters or so away, a narrow swath of plants still faintly pulses with delicate light—and life.

Except right before Shuri and K'Marah's eyes, row by row, the lights dim and go out.

A bright blur passes over a pocket of the remaining glowing herbs, obscuring them from view for the breadth of a second. The princess gasps and risks a peek at her Kimoyo card. "K'Marah, he's over there! Come on!"

They advance, carefully, quietly, the silence of their movement assisted by the sound-absorbing, Vibranium-soled shoes both girls are wearing. When Shuri tossed

K'Marah her auto-contouring pair, the to-be Dora looked at the toed slippers and said, "What are these, *feet gloves*?"

Now she's changed her tune. "These toe huggers are *amazing*, Shuri!" she says. "I can't hear a thing!"

"Shhh!"

As they get closer, the rows of light begin to fade more quickly.

"We won't make it in time," Shuri says, stopping their progress. "Here, give me the gauntlet. This should knock him unconscious, but if I need the other thing, you remember the code word, right?"

"Yep." K'Marah unslings the bag again, and the princess reaches in to pull out a boxing glove–style mechanized hand-covering that's shaped like a panther's paw. She shoves her fist inside.

"Here goes . . ." Shuri says.

And she lifts her arm, aims, and squeezes the trigger.

A shoot of brilliant light bursts forth, illuminating the entire field as it zips over the sea of shriveled herbs.

But then halfway across, the light hits something and, if Shuri's not mistaken, gets absorbed. She watches rapt as the light spreads from the center of the object out to its edges—the thing is shaped like a sun. But then the motion reverses: The light returns from each pointed tip to recondense in the center . . .

And the princess has fiddled with enough Vibranium-based tech to know exactly what that means.

"DUCK!" she shouts at K'Marah, grabbing hold of her friend's arm and yanking her to the ground just as the ray of electroluminescent kinetic energy comes back at them from the core of the sun-shaped shield.

"Oh my gods!" K'Marah exclaims. "What was *that*?"

"I'm not entirely sure, but whoever is wielding it certainly knows their way around our most valuable resource. That shield is made of Vibranium!"

"But how—"

"Princess Shuri, I am most surprised!" comes a familiar female voice that makes Shuri feel as though her very blood cells are quivering apart within her veins.

"No . . ." she whispers under her breath. Her hands go damp, and despite the glasses, her vision begins to cloud at the edges.

"Shuri?" K'Marah grabs her arm, snatching her back into the present. "Who *is* that? Why does she know your name?"

"Firing on an opponent whose back is turned? How very dishonorable! I expected better from you," the woman says.

Bright light suddenly fills the space from somewhere above Shuri's head. "Who are you, and what do you want?" K'Marah's voice booms. She's now standing, CatEyez removed, with her Kimoyo card held aloft, flashlight cranked up to full power.

The woman just smiles.

And even without the jagged teeth, red eyes, and scarily cracked skin, her visage is terrifying.

The woman from Shuri's worst nightmares is . . . larger than the princess would've expected. Taller than T'Challa, and with broader shoulders, her hair braided in thick cornrows, she's wearing an ornately embroidered stomach-baring top and billowing black trousers that taper at the ankles beneath a long, sheer kimono-style robe. The image of Wakanda being crushed in her (rather large) hand floats to the surface of Shuri's consciousness.

She's behind all this.

Shuri taps the left side of the glasses this time. A see-through blue screen appears before her eyes with the words *Search Mode* across the top. "I need to find out who that woman is and where she came from," the princess whispers.

The head of a panther spins in front of her eyes as the info-search begins, but then—

SPECTACLES OFFLINE. NO SIGNAL DETECTED.

"Well, that's just wonderf—"

"Henbane!" the woman shouts over her shoulder at the plant killer.

Shuri taps to return to night-vision mode (how primitive, that phrasing) and returns her focus to the woman.

"Come!" she continues to her crony. "There is someone I'd like for you to meet." Another smile.

As the person approaches—indeed, a boy who's long-limbed and deep brown–skinned, a hair taller than Shuri, and maybe a year older—the princess glances past him to the back corner of the field. The fading has slowed, but after a quick scan and mental calculation, Shuri is certain that within twelve to fifteen minutes, the last of the heart-shaped herb plants will succumb to whatever plague this *Henbane* has wrought upon them.

"Henny?" K'Marah says from beside her. The boy looks up and locks eyes with Shuri's friend. The princess turns to look at her as well—and instantly looks away. She's never seen K'Marah so angry. And hurt. "Or *Henbane*, I guess, is your real name? Why would you do this?"

Shuri's not sure whether her friend is talking about his active murder of the heart-shaped herb or his betrayal of *her*. But either way, she also wants to know.

"Ah, don't blame him," the woman says. "He was merely completing the job I hired him for. He was an aimless street urchin when I found him, but after all this is finished and I accomplish *my* mission, he'll be one of the richest and most powerful young men in the Horn of Africa."

The boy drops his head.

"For too long," the woman continues, "Wakanda has stood idly by, cloaked from view, while the rest of the region suffers from drought and rising temperatures. Our water has dried up. Our crops are failing. Our people are *dying* from heat exhaustion and dehydration—"

"Wait a minute! I know who you are!" K'Marah says. "You were at the Pan-African Congress on the Treatment of Superhumans!"

Shuri tries to ignore the surge of jealousy over this *second* Very Cool Congress Thing K'Marah has attended. (What even is the *point* of being a "princess"?)

"You're Princess Zanda of Narobia!" K'Marah goes on. "*You* were in support of that wretched Superhuman Registration Act from America!"

Princess Zanda continues to smile, but Shuri can tell it's forced now. "As Henbane here will tell you, we are very good to the *mutants* that live among us in Narobia."

(Shuri doesn't miss the extra emphasis on the *m*-word.)

"None of *this* would've been possible without him, in fact! Isn't that right, Henbane?"

The boy doesn't say a word.

"This gifted young man was discovered in the act of draining the life from a pawpaw tree behind the home of a Narobian diplomat. He was frail. Dry-skinned and brittle-boned. A beggar orphan en route to becoming a common criminal—or worse." She turns to Henny, whose narrow shoulders rise and fall with a sigh, though he still hasn't lifted his head. "In him, I saw great purpose. A sense of *destiny*. So I took him under my wing and we formed a grand plan that would shove this haughty and uncharitable nation from its self-erected pedestal."

Shuri flinches but doesn't respond.

Zanda goes on. "Knowing of the soft spot your countrymen seem to have for orphaned children—including children descended from pale-skinned monsters who would seek to keep our entire *continent* subjugated—Henbane entered this nation through the mountain region some time back, and was swiftly taken in by your Jabari."

Now Shuri is so baffled, she *has* to speak. *"Really?"*

"Told you they weren't so bad," K'Marah says from beside her. "Though *he* clearly is."

And then *he* speaks. "K'Marah, I'm—"

"Silence, Henbane," Zanda commands.

"But I need to tell her tha—"

"You need to tell her—them—nothing but 'Goodbye.'" She shifts her focus back to Shuri and K'Marah. "Your precious herb is *gone*, so once we eliminate that arrogant brother of yours, there will be no *Black Panther* strutting around with an unfair advantage. While your beloved king is engaged in that sham of a 'ritual Challenge'—as if any *normal* person could best a superhuman—the joined armies of we neighboring countries you neglect will invade this selfish nation. Troops have already begun their journey through a path our beloved Henbane set into motion through your border forest this morning."

Shuri shakes her head then. "They'll be stopped as soon as they cross the border. T'Challa already knows—"

"T'Challa knows NOTHING!" Zanda spits.

"Someone's delusional," K'Marah murmurs.

But Zanda rails on: "When I have secured access to your Vibranium and control over your goods and technology, I will be able to *assist* those who are suffering and dying in neighboring nations, as well as sell off some of your precious resources to interested buyers. I will appear to the wider world as wise, rich, *and* benevolent. And Narobia will finally receive the place of prominence it deserves on the international stage," she says, lifting her arms and sun shield into the air.

"Delusional," K'Marah says again.

Shuri risks a flick of her eyes past Zanda and sees that there are two rows of herbs left. Maybe ten plants total. She wishes she could focus there longer so she could estimate the rate at which they're fading into uselessness.

"Hey, S.H.U.R.I! What time is it?" Shuri shouts.

"The time is four thirty-seven p.m.," the voice replies from her Kimoyo card.

Twenty-three minutes until the Challenge—so eighteen before the path through the forest is clear and the armies break through.

Shuri plants her hands on her hips and shakes her head. "I could've sworn I set that *BLASTED* thing to the twenty-four-hour clock," she says.

Zanda cocks her head, momentarily thrown off—and successfully distracted—by the princess's bizarre declaration. Which gives K'Marah just enough time to react to the code word and toss Shuri the kitty cannon blaster prototype—a cat-shaped, handheld device that shoots bursts of electromagnetic energy from its open maw.

"K'Marah, kill the light!" Shuri fires off two shots—one at Zanda and one at Henbane—and because Zanda's sun shield is hanging at her side, she takes the hit right to the chest and cries out just as the field goes dark.

Henbane manages to dodge, the shot glancing off his right shoulder, but as Shuri takes off running in the direction of the remaining herbs, she hears a grunt and his voice shout, "Ow, not cool!" just before K'Marah says, "You sent me a *poisoned* bracelet? Really?"

Shuri manages a smile as she races toward the remaining plants . . . though what she plans to do when she gets to them, she doesn't know. There are seven herbs left, and as she runs, the number fades to six. Then the sixth one begins to fade. How is she supposed to *stop* something so clearly unstoppable?

So focused on the *what next?* is Shuri, she doesn't notice the figure who steps into her path until a beat too late. She runs smack into Zanda's sun shield and is subsequently blown back as the energy transferred to the shield in the collision is shoved back out into her chest.

All the air is knocked from her lungs when she hits the ground and her CatEyez tumble off. "Oof!" The back of her skull throbs—though she's sure the cushion of her giant bun of braids prevented an actual concussion—and spots appear in her line of vision.

By the time her head clears, there's someone standing over her.

"So young and overconfident," Zanda says, leaning down so Shuri has a better view of her face in the darkness. "Seems to run in the blood."

"Where"—Shuri coughs—"did you get that shield?"

Now Zanda laughs. "Henbane has been moving about your cherished nation for quite some time, Shuri. Poisoning your precious plants and shutting down a swath of the forest were aspects of his assignment, yes. But he learned a few other useful things as well."

"Henbane forged that shield?" As Shuri knows from her own work, crafting an object of that sort is no easy feat.

Pity. *Those* abilities would've been quite useful in a laboratory technician.

Shuri's head drops to the left, and that's when she sees it: one last heart-shaped herb plant still glowing bright. She stares, breath held as her heart sinks into the ground beneath her, awaiting the telltale fade of life.

Waiting . . .

But it doesn't come. The single stalk stays erect, a beacon of light in the darkness, both literal and figurative.

Zanda turns then, and Shuri gasps, cursing herself for her carelessness. "K'Marah—!"

"Henbane!"

They shout the names almost simultaneously, but K'Marah leaps into action first, her Kimoyo light re-illuminated and rigorous Dora Milaje training coming to the fore. Henbane, though, is right on her heels.

But then Zanda is up and headed toward the plant as well.

Shuri scrambles into action, sitting upright and feeling around on the darkened ground for her spectacles. She finds the little cannon blaster first. Knowing there's no time, as soon as her hand closes around it, she takes aim and fires, praying to Bast the shot doesn't hit K'Marah.

It goes wide, but the light from the blast glints off something shiny.

The glasses.

Shuri forces them onto her face and watches in horror as Henbane leaps toward her friend. "K'Marah!"

Shuri is on her feet and dragging her way forward.

And though Henbane barely grazes K'Marah's back with his fingertips, the Dora girl stumbles and collapses in a heap.

"I'm so sorry," Shuri hears him say as he drops to his knees beside her friend and lays a hand on her face. "I didn't have a choice. Zanda was going to kill my grandpapa . . . I left one plant alive—"

"Don't touch her!" Shuri fires another shot, and it hits him square in the left shoulder. He falls back, arm limp and useless at his side.

But it's too late: Zanda has reached the final herb. "Oh, Princess," she says, standing over it, as haughty and triumphant as Shuri's ever seen anyone look. "You try so hard. But as you Wakandans will have to learn: Sometimes failure is inevitable."

She reaches down and wraps a hand around the plant's stalk.

"STOP!" Shuri fires a shot at Zanda. Again the woman uses her shield to absorb and redirect the blow. The princess does her best to dodge, but it glances off her leg. "Ahhh!" She collapses as the entire left side of her body goes numb.

"Give UP, Princess!" Zanda shouts, reaching for the herb again.

"NO—"

But her cry is drowned out by an earth-trembling rumble of thunder.

Zanda freezes and looks skyward.

"Oh, you're in *big* trouble now," Shuri says, relief flooding every cell of her body.

Lightning flashes, and illuminated for the briefest of moments is a brown-skinned, white-haired woman, descending from the sky.

20

PRINCESS SHURI

And then the rain begins.

"Ororo!" Zanda shouts, releasing the herb and standing upright in evident panic. "What are *you* doing here?"

"Assisting my family," Storm says, white eyes blazing. "Shuri, you and K'Marah must get down to the baobab plain. The invading armies have broken through—"

"But T'Challa said we were prepared!" Shuri exclaims.

Zanda laughs, briefly distracted from her fear of the Mistress of the Elements. "Arrogant and witless, that T'Challa. Too full of self-importance to recogni—"

"Keep his name out of your wretched mouth!" Storm's eyes flicker, and a rogue gust of wind swirls around Zanda, twisting the thin fabric of her robe, and whipping her long braids into her face.

Shuri chuckles as she watches Zanda's arms flail about, but Ororo's sharp-edged voice brings her back to reality. "Your defenses were able to rout the ranks that made their way through the forest, Princess. But there were two other entry points, both of which went unguarded."

It clicks for Shuri then. "The forest entry was a diversion!"

"A successful one," Zanda shouts triumphantly from the midst of her personal tornado.

"Shut it!" Ororo flicks a hand in Zanda's direction, and the winds around her pick up speed.

"Gah!" Zanda shouts.

"Shuri, you and K'Marah must get down to the baobab plain to warn T'Challa. Two other factions have entered: one through the border with Azania, and one with Canaan. It would appear that both gained entry through tunnels."

"Tunnels?" Shuri says. "But how—" She looks over at where K'Marah is unconscious and Henbane is standing over her, very much not completing his task of killing the final herb. He looks up at Shuri. "Tunnels, too?" she says, and he averts his eyes. "K'Marah certainly knows how to pick a winner . . ." Shuri mumbles.

Henbane peeks over his shoulder at the still-struggling Zanda, then turns to Shuri. "I can wake her," he says, reaching for K'Marah.

"I told you not to touch her!" Shuri levels her cannon blaster at him again. "Get. Away."

He raises his working hand. The other arm is still limp and useless at his side.

"I'm sorry!" he says. "I didn't mean for things to go this far—" He shakes his head.

Shuri eyes him with suspicion. "How do I know you won't just hurt her more?"

"I didn't intend to hurt her at all. She's the only real friend I've ever had and . . . all of this was a mistake. I should not have responded to her message knowing of my mission—"

"Appreciate the heart-to-heart you kids are having, but *there is an invasion happening*. If you could wrap it up . . ." Ororo says.

Henbane drops down and runs his fingertips over K'Marah's cheek—and then quickly backs away.

Which is a smart move. Because as soon as she sits up, fully back to herself and looking like she just had the best night of sleep in her life, she's searching for him, eyes wide, rage heaving in her chest. "Where is he?"

"No time," Shuri says, pulling her friend to her feet and away from Henbane. She's more than a little nervous about what she plans to say to the boy, but there aren't any alternatives. So she steps right into his face. "If you're *really* sorry, and you care about her, protect that plant with your life."

"Huh?" K'Marah says. "If he—"

"We gotta move, K'Marah. Wakanda is under attack. We need to get to T'Challa."

As the *Predator* soars toward the site of the Challenge—which should be getting under way right about now—the girls pass over one of the other two entry points Ororo mentioned. The invading soldiers are flooding out of a hole in the ground at the edge of a patch of forest like deadly siafu ants fleeing a poked mound. Unable to just zip by as though nothing is happening, the princess pulls an astonishing midair U-turn and gets to firing round after round of bright-blue electromagnetic energy bursts into the ranks of interlopers. Depending on where they're hit, some are blown back, or trip and go sprawling, or are pulled to the ground when the arm holding their weapon goes limp, and gravity takes over.

"YES! Shuri! Knock them dead!" K'Marah shouts with a clap of her hands.

Of the soldiers who manage to evade Shuri's onslaught, only a handful refuse to abort their mission and attempt to press forward toward the baobab field. Most, however, scramble back to their entry point.

"Hold us steady," Shuri says, and K'Marah slides over to take the two-pronged steering mechanism. Then Shuri kneels down. "Full disclosure: I haven't actually tested this particular armament. It is very powerful and lined with Vibranium, and it utilizes kinetic energy collected in flight from contrary winds." There's a *chi-chock* sound as she loads the thing. "I call it the Imperial Blaster."

"Uhh . . ." is all K'Marah can muster.

"There will likely be a recoil."

She fires.

FWOOMP . . . BOOOOOOOM!

"Ahhh!" K'Marah screams and bounces into the air as the *Predator* jolts like someone smacked it on the rear.

"Sorry!" Shuri says, taking over the reins again. "Did the trick, though!"

And she's right: There may still be a tunnel beneath the forest floor, but it officially leads to a dead end—the blast remolded the earth and sealed off the exit.

"Onward!" Shuri says. "The guards near the Challenge grounds can handle the stragglers."

It takes three minutes for the girls to reach the edge of the baobab field. "Can you believe just two days ago we were looking down at a gathering of Wakanda's greatest warriors from that ridge over there?" K'Marah says, pointing. "And trying not to be seen?"

"Definitely feels like longer," Shuri replies, circling the perimeter of the field to prepare for landing.

Ororo revealed that she'd considered going to T'Challa herself, but with the Challenge looming, she felt that, as an outsider, interrupting the ritual would give the people of Wakanda the wrong impression. (Politics: barf.)

And though Shuri is a member of the royal family, something about Ororo's reasoning rings in her ears. The elders—Mother included—already feel the princess is frivolous. Adorable at times (she hates when they use that word, *adorable*, like she's one of the border clan's rhinoceros calves), but a nuisance at others.

She has a hunch that if she and K'Marah storm the plain, they'll be leaning into the latter, even if it *is* to shout that enemy forces have invaded.

Shuri parks the *Predator* not too far from the spot where they last laid eyes on T'Challa, and as they exit the vessel, they can hear the rhythmic rumble of drumbeats that precedes the tribal-clan roll call. They creep to where the land begins to slope gently downward, and then drop to a knee to avoid being totally conspicuous—two stalks, one long and reedy, the other short and stocky, but both stark against the horizon were one to look up in their direction.

"So what do we do now?" K'Marah whispers. The procession, where each clan of tribal representatives makes a grand entrance by heavily ornamented caravan, and then takes up their positions around the perimeter of the Challenge Ring—a glorified circle drawn on a patch of land where the grass doesn't grow—is ending as the final two delegations file into position to the beat of the drums. T'Challa has yet to make his grand appearance, but the girls can see the tent he will exit a few meters back from the edge of the ring.

"Oh look, there's Grandmother!" K'Marah says with a point and a smile.

Eldress Umbusi's shoulders and arms are bare, and the gold-and-bronze-threaded halter-tunic she's wearing makes her skin glow that much more. She looks . . . *radiant*. In fact, all the elders have come out in their finest, and from up here on the hill, the clumped clans look like precious gemstones, gathered in piles and glittering in the midafternoon sunlight—rubies, sapphires, emeralds, citrines, amethysts.

"We need to figure out—"

"Hey, S.H.U.R.I.," K'Marah says, "scan the perimeter."

"Scanning the perimeter," comes the reply.

"Hey, she's not supposed to respond to *you*," Shuri protests.

"Shhh."

There's a *ding*.

Shuri continues to scowl into the distance.

"Will you stop being ridiculous and check your Kimoyo card?"

"What for? We're supposed to be forming a plan—"

"So we can see where the final faction of invaders is coming from, duh!" K'Marah shakes her head. "You could never be a Dora Milaje."

"Oh, whatever." Shuri taps the screen of her Kimoyo card so that a hologram of their surroundings within a fifty-kilometer radius floats before their eyes. "There!" she exclaims, pointing out a gap in the woods to the northeast—and the insect-looking figures filing out of it. "That's about a half kilometer away—"

There's a loud and final *BOOM* from the drums, and then the whole plain goes silent. The girls watch the proceedings beneath them, now unable to pull their eyes away.

Okoye and Nakia, who are standing guard to either side of the tent's opening, turn to face each other with a snap.

Then T'Challa steps out.

"Great BAST!" Shuri's hands fly to her mouth, and she turns to K'Marah. "He's wearing the new *habit*! Your uncle must've completed and delivered it!"

Shuri watches spellbound as her unmasked brother, king, and protector of her and her people strides toward the circle. Okoye and Nakia fall into parallel rank a step behind him, staffs in opposite hands, chins slightly aloft. The silence—and reverence—are so absolute, it seems even the creatures of the air have ceased their movement.

A man approaches the opposite end of the Challenge Ring and bows. "My king," he says, loud enough for all to hear. "Thank you for your participation in this, our most sacred of traditions."

Uncle S'Yan.

His pride in his nephew resounds in his deeply resonant voice as he announces the rules of Challenge Day, and sets the ritual in motion.

As he paces around the outer rim of the Sacred Circle, addressing each tribe, drawing a smile here, a laugh there, a shallow bow or expression of sorrow over there . . .

"We have to take care of it," Shuri says, surprising even herself with the words.

"Huh?"

"The intruders." Shuri turns to K'Marah. "They timed this invasion to disrupt one of our oldest and most revered traditions. Distracted us with that forest move, thinking they'd hit us when our king's focus has shifted elsewhere, catch us off guard and use it to their advantage." Zanda's face flashes against the inside of Shuri's eyelids, but not the one from her vision—the one she's seen. That of a haughty—though clearly *delusional*—ruler who would attack a neighboring nation in a grab for power.

Shuri knows one thing: That's not the type of *princess* she ever intends to be.

"But they were wrong," she continues. "Our guard is *not* down, and we will not tolerate such blatant disrespect of our traditions. Which . . . make sense to me now. Even though before they sort of didn't."

K'Marah snorts. "So what's the plan, Your Majesty?"

Down below, Uncle S'Yan shouts, "Do we have a challenger? One who can prove themselves worthy by exhibiting readiness to lay his—or her—life on the line for the safety and welfare of Wakanda?"

Shuri smiles.

T'Challa pulls his mask on and steps into the circle.

"Let's go," Shuri says, not waiting to see if some brave warrior steps forward to face the Black Panther. "Can you pull up that terrain view again so we can send it to the *Predator*'s GPS? No need to send a king when a princess will do."

21

WAKANDA FOREVER

The plan forms as Shuri and K'Marah race back to the *Predator* and climb aboard.

And it's not foolproof. Especially considering how much of it will rely on prototype tech that hasn't been tested on the scale they're about to need it.

But as Shuri and her very best friend rise into the air inside a craft *she* built—a craft that has *safely* taken them from Wakanda to Kenya to London and back over the course of mere days—and she peeks down at the plain where her brother is flipping and kicking and dipping and dodging in the stretchiest suit a Black

Panther has ever known, a sense of purpose as thick and sweet as fresh mango juice slides down her throat and settles in her belly.

She's a princess, yes, but she was *made* to serve and protect her people.

"So where to first?" K'Marah says, taking over the role of navigator without being asked. She taps the map on the central screen, and a bird's-eye view of their immediate surroundings fills the cabin around them. Shuri uses her fingertips to rotate the landscape and zoom in on the target area. The interloping troops have formed ranks nine wide and seven deep . . . so far. There are still little insect-like specks filing out of a barely visible dark spot in a grove of trees.

With a clap, the map zooms out wide, and Shuri is able to see three things: (1) the triumphant group of Wakandan warriors returning from the hole in the forest after routing that particular group of invaders, (2) the captured men who managed to avoid being trapped in the second tunnel by Shuri's Imperial Blaster shot, and (3) a small faction of Wakandan warriors headed to face off against the group coming out of the third hole. As she and K'Marah watch, three figures in rhinoceros hats break off from the Wakandan ranks and run in the direction of the baobab field. Presumably to alert the king.

"Hey, S.H.U.R.I., how far to *this* spot?" Shuri pokes an area on the 3-D map, and it illuminates.

"Approximately twelve-point-eight kilometers, or three minutes and two seconds at the current rate of travel," the robot voice says.

Shuri rubs her chin. "And to the lab?"

"Twenty-three seconds southeast."

"So even with a stop, we could be there in five minutes," Shuri says to no one in particular.

K'Marah presses all ten fingertips together and then pulls them apart to zoom in on the skirmish at the border. The small contingent of Wakandans has reached the fray and is attempting to hold back the advancing army, but it's clear the rhino-hatted border guards could use some backup. If the princess had to guess, there's a good chance the best and brightest warriors were all sent to fight at the dying forest. Which would mean *these* were the guys . . . who were left. "You sure a pit stop is wise?"

Shuri turns the vessel away from the action. "Even if they trounce all of our guys and sprint full speed to the city, it would take a minimum of eleven minutes for the fastest person in the world to run that distance," Shuri says. "Zanda might've got them in—with advanced weaponry, from the looks of it . . ." Three tiny shoots of white light fly through the air from some miniature cannon thing and knock one of the border rhinos over on its side. Its legs continue to kick at the air. "But there are a couple of things she failed to consider."

"Yeah? Like what?"

"Well, *optimal mobility*, for one," Shuri says, gesturing with her chin at the enthusiastic, but discombobulated—and quickly tiring—invading soldiers as she lowers the *Predator* into the opening doors of her laboratory's hangar entrance.

"Noted," K'Marah replies with a nod. "And for two?"

When K'Marah looks over, Shuri is smiling. The princess presses a series of buttons and turns a few dials on the control panel before the rear hatch lowers. She rotates toward it and bounces on her toes.

"For two, she forgot to consider *me*," she says with a wink. "I'll be right back." And she disappears down the ramp and out of sight.

Shuri is back on the Predator, with an odd-looking half sphere in hand, quicker than K'Marah can blink, and within three and a half minutes, they're approaching what has literally become a battlefield. "Wow, that sure took a turn," K'Marah says as they get closer.

And she's not wrong: The number of interlopers

has . . . multiplied. To a point that seems, if not impossible, *highly* implausible.

"Where on earth did they all come from?" Shuri says to no one in particular.

"Well, looking at the map, I'd guess Niganda and Canaan," K'Marah says, bringing her palms together over the 3-D landscape to zoom out. "They're coming in beneath the part of the forest that borders on both countries. Is there a way to see the tunnel on this thing?"

Shuri nods and taps a screen to her left. The projected landscape turns white, and a long, thick red line appears at the southwest edge. "Infrared mode," she says. "It utilizes thermal readings and isolates—"

"Save it, Sherlock. We gotta stop this NOW. There are more of them coming." As K'Marah hyperzooms on the tunnel, Shuri sees exactly what she means: The thing is *full* of weapon-carrying men, three flush in a line that extends a quarter of the distance to the border—which is over a kilometer and a half away.

Shuri gulps. She's tempted to ask her AI for a count of the intruders—there have to be over a thousand—but decides against it. Maybe better not to know *exactly* what they're up against.

"We do have a plan . . ." K'Marah looks up, panic splashed over her face like a hastily thrown cup of ice water. "Right?"

Shuri continues to stare at the holographic rendering of a piece of her homeland she's never even seen up close. How many other corners of Wakanda has she yet to explore? How many treasures has she yet to find?

What will happen if she fails at *this* mission?

"Shuri?" K'Marah's dread is palpable now.

Shuri *cannot* fail. She *must* not.

She can *do* this. She can beat them.

She can.

She just hopes all the Wakandans who answered the call to defense did so because they were wearing their communication bracelets.

"Hey, S.H.U.R.I., highlight all the Kimoyo beads within this region." Shuri circles the area on the map where most of the moving bodies are gathered. A few stragglers have made their way farther in, but for the most part, the Nigandans/Narobians/Canaanites/*whoever* haven't made a ton of progress in their march on the city.

"Highlighting Kimoyo beads," the AI says.

About a hundred of the mini people on the map turn purple . . . and not all of them are in motion.

K'Marah gasps. "Are those ones—"

"Let's not think about it right now," Shuri says, stepping up to the *Predator*'s control panel. She manually shifts into hover mode, and the aircraft slows to a stop with the thick of the melee still a couple of hundred meters or so in front of them. Then she slides to the left and pushes a button. A hidden screen flips into view, and she taps a series of numbers into it before a lever slides out of a concealed slot in the ceiling.

"Sheesh, how many secret doodads does this thing have?"

Shuri grins at her friend, confidence renewed. "If only you knew," she says. "Hey, S.H.U.R.I., activate Kimoyo Capture."

"Kimoyo Capture activated." All the purple people turn green.

She cautiously wraps a hand around the lever then. And takes a deep breath. "You, uhh, might want to buckle up," she says to K'Marah.

"Why?" (Though the shorter girl scrambles into the co-captain's chair and fastens herself in before Shuri has a chance to answer.)

"There might be a small jolt. Though it'll be way worse for *them* . . ."

"WAI—"

Shuri shoves the lever forward—

And is almost thrown back as every human body below with a Kimoyo bead attached to it is wrapped in a tiny force field and pulled three or so meters into the air, out of the reach of enemy hands.

"By *BAST*!" K'Marah gasps. She turns to Shuri, thunderstruck. "I guess that *does* come in handy! How does it work again?"

Shuri reaches forward with her free hand and turns a dial. The bodies begin to move toward them *very* quickly—"Whoops! Too fast!" she says—then slower as she reverses the dial the slightest bit. She and K'Marah can both see some of the person-filled bubbles shifting shape as the inhabitants squirm and flail within them. "It's a simple mechanism, really," she begins. "I use the Kimoyo tech to create an electromagnetic field around each individual utilizing their body heat—"

"Nope, never mind." K'Marah lifts a hand. "What next?"

"Well, uhhh . . ." Shuri focuses in on a section of the map projection . . . but doesn't let go of the lever or the dial. She glares at it for a moment, narrowing her eyes.

"Umm, Shuri? Hello? Next?"

The princess's forehead wrinkles as her concentration intensifies.

And then her face goes slack and she drops her chin. "Can you take your finger and circle that open area on the other side of the stream we just crossed? South of the baobab plain."

K'Marah doesn't respond, and when Shuri looks

up, she sees that her dear friend is smirking. "You can't let go of those things, huh, genius?"

"I truly despise you sometimes."

K'Marah does as Shuri requested, snickering the whole time, and as soon as all the floating Wakandan soldiers have entered the target area—as indicated by a *ding* and the space turning yellow on the floating map—Shuri cranks the dial to zero, carefully lets go, and then slowly pulls the lever back to lower the soldiers back down.

The force fields vanish, and both girls watch, relieved, as most of the little figures plop to the ground, then stagger to their feet, confused but safe.

"Whew!" Shuri says, lifting her hand for K'Marah to high-five. "Phase one complete." She spreads her arms wide and brings her hands together in a clap. The map folds and vanishes, returning the cabin to its *regular* overly high-tech state, then Shuri turns back to the control panel, shifts out of hover mode, and eases them into motion in the direction of the invaders.

"Let me guess: Phase one was the easy part," K'Marah says, coming to stand at Shuri's side.

"Mmmm . . . You could say that."

"Figures."

The girls lapse into silence as the horde of invaders comes into full view before them.

"There are so *many*," K'Marah continues, breathless.

Shuri doesn't respond to that. She just begins a slow descent over the re-forming ranks, shifting into hover when they're right over the center.

"We're invisible right now, yes?" K'Marah asks.

"Yes," Shuri says with a confident nod.

But then she looks down.

It would seem the invaders have been reenergized by the whisking away of Wakanda's warriors. As they re-form their ranks and march onward, they hit their shields against their chests and chant some kind of battle cry.

It shakes the princess. "K'Marah?"

"Whatever you're planning, it's going to work." The soon-to-be Dora turns to Shuri and puts a hand on her friend's shoulder. "Okay?"

Shuri's heart rate increases, and she faces back forward. Her eyes sweep the masses below again, and she opens her mouth to speak, but all that comes out is a strange squawk she had no idea her throat could make.

"Maybe it'll help if you . . ." K'Marah takes an audible centering breath. ". . . explain the science of your plan. To me."

And then the world opens and a light turns on. "Really?" Shuri says.

"Mm-hmm!" K'Marah forces a smile.

Which is more than enough for the princess. Setting her nerves on a back burner, she kicks into high gear. "Okay, so I've been secretly working on some new security tech." She squats and pulls a rounded, though flat-bottomed, black object etched with glowing purple lines from a compartment beneath the control panel. "This hemisphere," she says, holding it up, "is what I returned to the lab to retrieve. I call it the Dome. It's merely a prototype, but my hope is that through the use of a spectrometer, I will be able to mimic its shape and create an impenetrable force field around a predetermined area."

She tucks the half sphere under one arm and, with brows pinched and tongue poking out, begins to tap, pinch, shift, and slide her fingers around the main navigation screen. When there's a perfect circle encompassing the tunnel exit *and* all the foreign soldiers—which is easier than she expected it to be considering their insistence on moving in ranks—she nods with satisfaction. Then she drops down again, lifts a hatch in the floor, and lowers the glowy purple-black thingy into it.

She closes the compartment, and stands. Returns to her controls. "If this works like I hope it will, the spectrometer will create the parameters, and the Vibranium released from the Dome will follow the photonic pathway and bind with the carbon molecules along it.

Creating . . . a dome. The intruders will be trapped inside."

"Oh! Like a high-tech snow globe!" K'Marah looks ready to burst, she's so excited to understand.

"Precisely!" Shuri says.

"And then what?"

"And then T'Chal—I mean, the king . . ." Shuri steels herself. They've been so busy, she has no idea if he won the Challenge. "The king can decide what to do with them."

K'Marah nods. "Excellent plan." Then she turns to the princess. "So you ready?"

Shuri presses a button beneath the center of the control panel, and two little doors slide open as another hidden lever rises up. She grabs hold of it. "I was born ready."

"YOU TOTALLY WATCH AMERICAN MOVIES, TOO!" K'Marah shouts.

Shuri smirks.

And shoves the lever forward.

Neither girl speaks as the Dome descends, but Shuri *knows* it is by far the coolest thing she's ever created. They watch as what looks like a flickering liquid pours down over an invisible, upside-down bowl. Even the invading troops look up in awe.

There's a *ding* before the S.H.U.R.I.'s voice rings

out. "Dome deployment complete," it says.

Shuri and K'Marah look at each other.

"Is that . . . it?" the Dora says.

"Guess there's only one way to find out."

Shuri sets the *Predator* down a reasonable distance away: close enough to investigate and get back to the vessel quickly if need be, but far enough away to give them a head start if they have to flee.

Then they get out.

"Here goes," Shuri says, prepping her Kimoyo bracelet to fire temporary-paralysis pulses from the inside of the wrist, spider guy style just in case.

"Shuri . . . look," K'Marah says, pointing. She turns to the princess with a smile.

And Shuri can't help but smile back. Because it's clear from the men banging on the inside of the invisible structure, creating little outward ripples of light (perhaps she should electrify the thing?), that they're trapped inside.

It worked.

"You did it!" K'Marah says, leaping onto her friend.

Shuri barely catches the shorter girl. "*WE* did it." The girls hug. "You and me. Together—"

"Guess that means you should be punished together, eh?" comes a familiar voice from behind them.

Shuri shuts her eyes.

"Oh boy," K'Marah says.

"Lies upon lies upon lies. I don't know what's gotten into you, Shuri, and I am much too civilized to try to paddle it out. But know that you have quite a bit of explaining to do—"

"You too, K'Marah!" comes a second adult female voice.

"Ugh," K'Marah sighs. "Guess I'm in trouble, too."

"Likely," Shuri says.

And then she takes a deep breath. "Turn around and face the music on three?"

"Let's just get it over with . . ."

So both girls turn. And as they look into the furious faces of the queen mother and Eldress Umbusi, they know: The battle might have been won, but the war has yet to begin.

MISSION LOG

I AM "GROUNDED." (CLEARLY EVEN MOTHER CAN'T RESIST AMERICAN TELEVISION SHOWS ON PANTHERTUBE.)

Indefinitely, was the answer I received when I asked, "For how long?" but considering the success of my Dome technology and the fact that our Ministry of Defense is now clamoring to figure out how to expand it—the mechanized forest has been deemed "insufficient security" after the events of Challenge Day—I'm certain this bizarre punishment won't last for long.

While K'Marah and I were trying to save the nation, three brave souls stepped forward to challenge T'Challa. And in his new kinetic-energy absorbing, hyperstretchy Panther Habit, he trounced them all.

Was our *king* stunned to regain access to his technology and immediately learn that over the course of the seventeen-minute Challenge, a full-on ground invasion *had* taken place? Yes.

But he was also grateful. For me. His darling "zeal"-filled baby sister who clearly has more "wisdom and foresight" than he possesses in his little finger. SO grateful was he, in fact, he convinced Mother of my need for tactical, weapons, and combat training.

In regard to the foreign troops: The sixteen or so that managed to progress ahead of the others were all caught and arrested. The ones *within* the Dome were so shaken by first seeing the Wakandan warriors literally lifted from the fray, carried away in midair, and then finding themselves entrapped within a structure that came down around them like a lowering glass goblet, none of them moved when the Dome vanished, and Wakanda's finest warriors—led by the Dora Milaje, of course—surrounded them on all sides. T'Challa said many of them bowed to him as he approached, convinced he was a god. (Like his head needs to be any bigger.)

After confiscating their weapons and having their hands bound, T'Challa had them escorted back to the tunnel in groups of thirty and let them leave the way they had come.

I'm sure—as he is—that they won't return.

And thanks to Ororo, Zanda was placed in a capsule with her very own tornado swirling around her, and hand-delivered to the Narobian capital. She'll be fine provided they figure out how to extract her without unleashing the live cyclone on the city.

Henbane has been detained and is awaiting trial. There was, of course, more to his story than Zanda let on: While he *was* discovered in the act of killing some rude rich man's mango trees, he only took the "job" with Zanda because she claimed she could connect him with members of the family he's never known.

When she purported to have discovered a grandfather of his, he latched on like a drowning man to a life preserver, so desperate was he for family. He did everything she asked of him, despite the fact that she continued to pile on demands that had to be met before she'd "reunite" them.

He got suspicious, of course. But then she began to threaten first Henbane, then this grandpapa, with death if Henny didn't do precisely as she directed. And at that point, what could he have done? Even if there was no grandpapa (and unfortunately, there wasn't), he was in too deep. Zanda was the *ruler* of Narobia, and Henbane is only fourteen.

But the interesting twist: that final herb? He deliberately left it alive. It remained when we returned to the Sacred Field.

Which brings me to the real reason for this log: Through a bit of trial and error over the past few days, I just figured out a way to rid the heart-shaped herb cells of Henbane's toxin—which, it turns out, is a mutated version of the poison

found in the plant from which "Henbane"
derived his name (his given name is Larry,
apparently).

Long story short, by immersing the desiccated roots in a hypertonic solution
made of water and the fishy-smelling goop
I extracted from previous plants (of all
things!), I'm able to stimulate osmosis
and force the toxin out. Then after a
time in a *hypo*tonic solution of water
that has been purified through *reverse*
osmosis and infused with Vibranium, the
cells fix themselves.

It will take a while to regrow a solid
crop, but that's okay.

For now, our nation's (pssst . . . *my*)
future is safe.

Wakanda forever.

NIC STONE

is the *New York Times* bestselling author of the novels *Dear Martin* and *Odd One Out*. She was born and raised in a suburb of Atlanta, Georgia, and the only thing she loves more than an adventure is a good story about one. After graduating from Spelman College, she worked extensively in teen mentoring and lived in Israel for a few years before returning to the United States to write full-time. Having grown up with a wide range of cultures, religions, and backgrounds, she strives to bring diverse voices and stories into her work. Learn more at nicstone.info.